Benson jumped for the window.

Out there, hanging onto no visible support at all, as far as could be seen, was a sort of mad gorilla form. A man, yet with the face of an insane beast, dressed in clothes that were burned and torn till they were little more than rags.

"Nevlo!" panted Blake.

The hideous face disappeared. Benson got the window up and looked down in time to see the crooked form drop to the sidewalk, knock down several screaming pedestrians, and then disappear from sight.

A madman with power to shake the world was on the loose! NEVLO

Other Books

In This Series

By Kenneth Robeson

AVENGER #1: JUSTICE, INC.
AVENGER #2: THE YELLOW HOARD
AVENGER #3: THE SKY WALKER
AVENGER #4: THE DEVIL'S HORNS
AVENGER #5: THE FROSTED DEATH
AVENGER #6: THE BLOOD RING
AVENGER #7: STOCKHOLDERS IN DEATH
AVENGER #8: THE GLASS MOUNTAIN
AVENGER #9: TUNED FOR MURDER
AVENGER #10: THE SMILING DOGS
AVENGER #11: THE RIVER OF ICE
AVENGER #12: THE FLAME BREATHERS
AVENGER #13: MURDER ON WHEELS
AVENGER #14: THREE GOLD CROWNS
AVENGER #15: HOUSE OF DEATH
AVENGER #16: THE HATE MASTER

Published By
WARNER PAPERBACK LIBRARY

the Avenger

NEVLO
by Kenneth Robeson

WARNER PAPERBACK LIBRARY

A Warner Communications Company

WARNER PAPERBACK LIBRARY EDITION
FIRST PRINTING: OCTOBER, 1973

COPYRIGHT © 1941 BY STREET & SMITH PUBLICATIONS, INC.
COPYRIGHT RENEWED 1969 BY THE CONDÉ NAST PUBLICATIONS, INC.
ALL RIGHTS RESERVED

THIS WARNER PAPERBACK LIBRARY EDITION IS PUBLISHED
BY ARRANGEMENT WITH THE CONDÉ NAST PUBLICATIONS, INC.

COVER ILLUSTRATION BY GEORGE GROSS

WARNER PAPERBACK LIBRARY IS A DIVISION OF WARNER BOOKS, INC.,
75 ROCKEFELLER PLAZA, NEW YORK, N.Y. 10019.

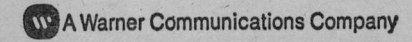

A Warner Communications Company

NEVLO

CHAPTER I

Dedication

It was one of the most beautiful spots in Ohio.
There was a good-sized river rushing merrily down from smooth green hills; there was a gorge, an increase in the speed of the current. There were woods and large, well-kept farms on the banks of the river.

Then there was the new power plant.

The power plant did not detract from the loveliness of the scenery too much. It was a symmetrical and well-designed structure that seemed to nestle at the foot of a tree-clad hill as if it belonged there. The dam, sprawling from its flank, made a pleasing waterfall.

The plant was just outside the little town of Marville. It was one, the newest, link in the chain of power-generating stations owned by the Grant Utilities Corp. Its name was simply Plant 4.

Marville and the surrounding Ohio section was proud of Plant 4. Naturally, the people hereabouts, and the possessing corporation, Grant Utilities, could not know that Plant 4 was destined to become a jinx on an almost international scale.

They all looked at the new, solid building and beamed like fond parents on a child prodigy.

Plant 4 had the newest and biggest and best in equipment. It would supply power to several thousand square miles, all the way north to Cleveland, replacing four or five obsolete local plants.

And everybody of local importance was out here today to do it official honor.

"Got a nice day for it, too," said the editor of the Marville *Journal,* present with all the other celebrities.

"Yeah, swell," said the man next to him, a Marville store-owner.

It was a nice day. The sun shone brightly, and the rushing river that was to whirl the giant turbines and light and power a large community looked like an animated string of blue diamonds.

"There's the mayor. They're all going inside."

The editor of the Marville *Journal* nodded, and he and the store-owner moved in with the several dozen other notables to the cathedral-like interior of the plant.

They're clean and bare and seemingly empty, these new power plants. There are half a dozen great generators, a flock of gargantuan switchboards, a few electric cables like ships' hawsers, and that's about all.

In the sunny, clean vastness of Plant 4, the local notables seemed lost. But they acted extra pompous to overbalance their physical tininess.

And no one was more pompous than Mayor Bristow. He stood near the big switchboard containing the master switch, and beside him stood Blake, president of Grant Utilities Corp.

John Blake, large, solemn-looking, middle-aged magnate, was in the corporation's main offices in Cleveland far more than he was in Marville. But he had a home here, and he was, of course, here on the occasion of the dedication of Plant 4.

Next to Blake was the young engineer in charge, Bill Burton.

Burton, young, husky, with thick brown hair that was always rumpled and out of place, looked like a young hen viewing its first egg. This was his first executive job.

Engineer-in-charge, president of corporation owning the plant, the mayor, notables—all was as it should be. But over at one fringe of the crowd . . .

"Oh-oh!" said the editor of the Marville paper, in a low voice. "The ghost at the feast!"

Near one of the thirty-foot windows looking out over the Marville River was a tall man with black hair that had a gray streak in it, and with black, biting eyes.

The eyes viewed the crowd of notables as if pouring acid over them. The man's mouth was twisted in a bitter, crooked line. He held his large head a bit to one side, as if studying the personages with malicious intensity. But that was not the reason. He always held his head to one side, had always carried it that way as far back as his oldest friend could remember.

"I'll say—the ghost at the feast!" the store-owner whispered back to the editor, staring at the black-eyed man next to the lofty window. "Nevlo, himself. Funny that he's allowed in here at such a time."

"It would be awkward to try to keep him out," shrugged the editor. "After all, Nevlo was chief engineer in the Marville section for the corporation for many years. He designed Plant 4, when you come right down to it. He's responsible for all this stuff that's about to be dedicated."

"But he was fired a month ago," protested the store-owner.

"So he was fired a month ago," said the editor, shrugging again. "And he's so sore-as-a-boil he'd like to pour emery dust in the generator bearings. But Blake still couldn't quite bar him out of here without its looking bad. As I said, Nevlo is the man whose brain child this plant really is."

"Wonder how young Burton feels about all this?"

"Burton is okay," said the editor. "He's a right guy. Nice youngster. He feels badly about Nevlo's being canned. He didn't want to take another man's job. But when the president discharges a man and appoints you in his place, what is there to do but obey orders?"

"Can he fill Nevlo's shoes?"

"Sure! He's a good engineer—Ssh! They going to begin."

His Honor, Mayor Bristow, cleared his throat pompously and loudly. It had the effect of a banging gavel in the hands of an assembly leader about to open a session, or of a warning bell as a school class is about to begin.

Everyone turned toward Bristow.

"Gentlemen," boomed the professionally oratorical voice, "we are gathered here at this most auspicious occasion—"

The booming voice, saying nothing in particular but saying it in ringing, earnest tones, filled the big room like the humming of a bluebottle fly. Smooth, even, soothing. The men present kept from yawning and politely applauded now and then. The mayor's hand caressed the master switch, which it would throw in a few minutes.

And over near the window, a bitter-looking, black-haired man, who habitually held his head slanted to the left, gazed with sardonic amusement. Nevlo, the man whose brain had spawned this place, but whose ungovernable temper and erratic lack of a sense of responsibility had gotten him discharged.

In spite of the mayor's windy nothings, the air of the place began to grow more tense as he neared the peak of his speech—and the moment when he would throw that switch.

There began to be quite a little suspense in the wait

for the movement of the switch. Then, light would gleam, and current would flood cables and take over the work of the obsolete plants dotted from twenty to sixty miles away from Plant 4.

A big occasion, a smooth and sleek occasion . . .

"Wouldn't it be funny," whispered the editor suddenly, "if the damn thing didn't work, after all."

The store-owner stared at him, almost shocked. Then he grinned a little.

"Don't be silly. The turbines, generators—everything here has been checked a dozen times. There isn't a chance of its not working."

"I know," said the editor. "There isn't, really."

"And so, fellow citizens," the mayor boomed along, "in dedicating this edifice to the use of mankind, we are sanctioning the functioning of a true work of creation. When this switch is pressed, light shall leap into being throughout this great room—and in thousands of homes through our glorious state. When these great wheels begin to turn, the wheels of countless factories will turn with them. And all resulting from the movement of one man's hand. My hand, gentlemen. I am highly honored to be the man who moves this switch!"

There was a breathless five seconds. Every eye was on the switch and on the rows of light bulbs set nearby. Every ear was on the alert to catch the slowly gathering humming of the great generators. There was silence in the place so complete that the slamming of the master switch sounded like a pistol shot.

And then there was a silence even more complete.

The generators started their humming, all right. The hum changed to a shrill whine of great speed.

But nothing else happened. The lights didn't glow at all. They stayed cold and dead, though presumably current was shooting through them with the switch contact.

River rushing, turbines whirling, generators whining—and nothing was coming of it.

Over near the tall window sounded a bitter sardonic laugh. And that cracked the silence.

"Hey," said the mayor, staring at the lights that didn't light, "did I do something wrong?"

Young Burton, staring pop-eyed at the switchboard, went white and leaped for Bristow's side. After him, only a little less hurriedly, came President Blake.

Burton batted the mayor's fumbling hand away from the switch and took over himself. He pulled it down and snapped it back several times.

And nothing happened!

It was something more than disconcerting. It was like proudly breaking the bottle of champagne over the nose of a ship and then having the ship stay on the ways and refuse to slide down to the sea.

A fine new plant, this Plant 4—only it didn't work.

Blake was observed to say something out of the corner of his mouth to Burton, and the engineer grew even whiter. Then Blake, sleek, efficient, smiling, faced the rest.

"It seems a slight mechanical defect has ruined our dedication," he announced, with just the right amount of rueful humor. "We'll have to accept the dedication and start the wheels turning in a few hours, when adjustments have been made. For, of course, in a few hours—"

"This plant will never generate any power!"

The mayor's voice had sounded loud when he orated. Blake's had sounded assured when he spoke of minor adjustments.

This voice seemed to fill the place like an explosion, and it was more assured than Blake's had ever been.

It came from Nevlo, the big, blazing-eyed man near

the window. Nevlo, who had designed the plant and had been fired a month before its opening.

"What did you say, Nevlo?" snapped Blake, face first red and then chalky with fury.

"I said Plant 4 will never generate power. Not till I am in charge again."

Blake nodded to a couple of huskies in dungarees.

"Throw him out if he doesn't get out by himself."

"Oh, I'll get out!" said Nevlo. "And you'll want me to come back, and you'll beg me to come back, many times before I do. For I tell you this plant will never function till I allow it to."

Head to one side, lips stony in their bitterness, Nevlo left the plant. Blake faced the rest, managing an artificial smile.

"You can disregard the vindictive mutterings of a man discharged for incompetence," he said. "And you may also disregard his vague threats about Plant 4. I'm not much of an engineer, but I know that no power on earth can keep these generators from doing their job as long as the river turbines turn them."

Which was true enough, it seemed. Burton, himself, reassured Blake, when the rest had gone and the two were left alone beside the great generators that were whirling so industriously—and were producing nothing.

"Sure," he said, biting his lips, "that's right, Mr. Blake. As long as these generators are turning, power is sent over the cables."

"They're turning, and there is no power," Blake snapped.

"There must be something physically wrong with the set-up," worried Burton. "Some little thing, though I can't imagine what. I checked everything dozens of times."

"Can there be anything to what Nevlo said? Is it possible that he could get revenge by sabotaging the plant?"

"No man could keep a whirling generator from building up power," swore Burton.

"Well, these are whirling," said Blake again. "And it doesn't mean anything. You'd better find out what's wrong, my young friend, or I'll fire you faster than I fired Nevlo, and I'll see that you don't get a job with another utility company in the continent!"

So Burton, thick brown hair more rumpled than ever, checked Plant 4 again. And again he found that everything was exactly as it should be. Wiring okay, turbines okay, generators okay. And from this shining, whirling, perfect generating unit, not one bit of juice emerged.

Nevlo's bitter, assured laugh rang in his ears again and again, though he *knew* no man could revoke the fundamental laws of electricity as they seemed to have been revoked here. So he checked and searched and grew haggard and found only perfection. And Nevlo's black eyes haunted him.

That was in March, five weeks before the series of events that shook the world.

CHAPTER II

Blackout!

The drugstore on Sixth Avenue looked like any other drugstore on Sixth Avenue. Or any other avenue. That is, it looked that way from the front.

There were counters behind which were all the thousand and one items carried by modern drugstores. There was a prescription counter along one side. A gleaming soda fountain ranged along the other side.

At the soda fountain sat a customer, a Negro, gangling, lean, looking sleepy and stupid.

But this was Josh Newton, graduate with high honors from Tuskegee and an aid of Richard Henry Benson, known to the underworld as The Avenger.

And the store, with its normal, ordinary look, was just as deceptive as Josh Newton. For it wasn't ordinary at all. You could have found that out by going into the rear room.

The rear room was twice as big as the front. And it had no store supplies. It was a dual laboratory, with chemical apparatus on one side and electrical on the other.

The chemical side was the property of Fergus MacMurdie. The electrical apparatus was presided over by Algernon Heathcote Smith. These were two more of The Avenger's aides. They were both engaged in experiments at the moment.

Smitty worked with his back turned to MacMurdie. And a tremendous back it was. Smitty was a six-foot-nine, near-three-hundred-pound giant, with all of it muscle and bone. No one would have divined from his moonface —more amiable than intelligent—that he was one of the world's outstanding electrical engineers.

"*Whoosh*! 'Tis the devil has got ye!" Mac suddenly howled, throwing a beaker half full of pinkish stuff to the floor.

"You sandy-thatched Scotch ram," Smitty snapped. "Why're you throwing junk all around the place?"

"It's not junk. It's my new local anesthetic. A drop of it blocks all sensation for an hour and a half. Put it on a finger and ye could cut the finger off without pain. Apply it to the gum around a sore tooth, and ye could yank the tooth without feelin' it. 'Tis an invaluable thing."

"So you go throwing it around the shop," said the giant. "I can see how invaluable it is."

The Scot chewed his lips, his bleak blue eyes glaring.

"Ye overgrown papoose. It *is* invaluable!"

"But?"

"Well," admitted Mac, "'tis a wee bit strrrong, right now. It seems to kill flesh a little bit, as well as pain. I've got to take the bite out of it. I thought I had, and it seemed I hadn't; so I got a trifle impatient."

"Nice stuff," approved Smitty. "You put it on a finger to kill pain, and it kills the finger."

"*Whoosh*!" grated Mac. "And what're ye workin' on? A set of buildin' blocks?"

It was the giant's turn to be stung.

"I'm working on something *really* important, if you want to know," he rapped out. "A new heating element that will take a five-hundred-percent overload without burning out, will be indestructible, and can be cheaply made. It will be—"

"Children's play," scoffed Mac. "Ye don't lose yer temper because ye never have sufficient cause, what with your little experiments. I'm going to buy ye an electric train for next Christmas. Ye'll love it, Algernon."

"Why, you—" began Smitty, outraged.

Mac got out of there. He was one of the few mortals on earth who could call Smitty by his given name and not be torn to bits. But there was no use pushing his luck too far.

He went gloomily into the front part of the drugstore and replaced his bright-eyed assistant behind the soda fountain. There, he watched sourly while Josh Newton finished his fifth maple-nut sundae.

"If ye were a payin' customer," he remarked bitterly, "I could retire with a fortune in a year. But we both work for Muster Benson, and so ye come in here and lap up them sundaes on the house."

Josh grinned. Mac didn't have to watch the pennies, but it was deeply ingrained in his Scottish nature to do so.

A youngster came in and ordered a chocolate malted milk. Mac mixed it and set the chromium beaker on the little stand for the electric mixer to take over. The busy whir of the mixer rose.

"I will have," began Josh, "another maple-nut sundae with lots of nuts—"

He stopped. The mixer had stopped, and the lights in the store had gone out.

There was a howl from the rear, indicating that whatever Smitty was working on had been forced to a halt because of failure of electric current.

"Must have blown the main fuse down in the basement," said Mac. "I'll go—"

The lights went on again, and the mixer started its whirring. About twenty seconds had passed.

"Hm-m-m! Powerhouse failure," said Mac, not very disturbed. No presentiment of the extent of the thing that had just happened occurred to him. Not just then.

Smitty came barging out, looking like a bull on a rampage.

"What did you do," he raged, "pull the switch in the basement? I ought to take some of your own half-baked local anesthetic and pour it over your head—"

"Mac didn't do anything," said Josh. Inasmuch as there was no one in the store but the youth who had ordered the chocolate malted, he didn't bother to talk as a black man is expected to talk. He only saved his drawl for public places, as protective coloration. With friends, he spoke as crisply and precisely as any college professor.

"All right," snapped the giant Smitty, "if Mac didn't haul the juice out of my experiment, what did?"

"A transformer down the line must have blown out," shrugged Josh. "Or else there was a power-plant failure for a few seconds."

"Well, if that was all—" Smitty began.

A man came hurriedly into the drugstore. The man had on a worn brown suit and a taxi-driver's cap.

"Got a phone, pal?" he asked Mac.

"Booth in the rear, left side," said Mac.

The man started for it. Another cab-driver hurried in. He nodded to the first.

"After you on the phone, Joe. Got a little ignition trouble, and I want to give the shop fits about it. The idea, sendin' a guy out with a can that goes dead on him—"

"Did your heap go dead, too?" asked the first man.

"Yeah! Yours?"

"Uh-huh! I can't find anything wrong, either. Points all right, plugs okay, battery up—"

Smitty had been listening more and more intently. He broke in now.

"Both your cabs went dead?" he said.

The two drivers looked him up and down.

"That's right, Sampson," Joe said.

"When was this?"

"Just a coupla minutes ago."

"Let's go out, now," suggested Smitty, "and see if they're still dead."

"Look! Don't you think we guys know something about ignition—"

"It won't hurt to shove down on the starter, will it?" said Smitty.

So they went out. And Joe got into his cab and pressed the starter. The starting motor hummed merrily, and the cab engine started.

So did the other man's.

"That," said Joe slowly, "is doggone funny!"

Smitty's eyes were round with amazement and with a dawning, vague horror. To him, it was something far more than peculiar.

For fifteen or twenty seconds the juice had been cut off in Mac's store. Nothing startling about that. But it began to seem that during those seconds these two cars at the curb had had their ignition systems go dead, too.

And the little power plants of the taxis had nothing whatever to do with the big power plant that supplied juice to Mac's drugstore, along with thousands of other buildings.

He turned and strode back into the store.

"Mac, there's something pretty fishy going on. Try to get the chief on the phone, will you? I'll be back with a report in a little while."

The giant began an investigation that made his eyes pop out more and more as it proceeded.

He talked to bus-drivers. For a few seconds their buses had gone dead. Traffic cops told him that the Stop-and-Go lights had gone out for a little while. They guessed the power plant had a breakdown, and the juice had failed till emergency generators could be hooked in.

He phoned to widely separated points on Manhattan Island, covered by three or four plants. It developed that for those few curious seconds the whole island was without power.

He went to the docks. A tugboat captain said his engines had gone dead. He phoned Newark and Long Island, powered by still other plants. Same story. He contacted Pennsylvania, Chicago, Denver, Toronto.

And the thing grew and grew till, to a man with an electrical training like Smitty's, it took on colossal, nightmare proportions.

He radioed a liner just off the three-mile limit. Its power had gone dead for a few seconds; the chief engineer was unable to explain why. Not till Smitty had contacted a ship a hundred and ten miles out did the story vary. This ship had had no trouble.

He came back to Mac's drugstore as if the devil were after him and galloped into the back room.

"Muster Benson's on the radio, now," Mac said from beside a big cabinet at the rear of the room.

The large cabinet contained the last word in television radios, far beyond anything the commercial laboratories had as yet devised.

On the screen was a face. It was a very young face for a man so famous, so eminent in almost any profession, for a man who had accomplished so very much in every corner of the world. But Dick Benson had crowded a full, prosperous and adventurous life into his early years and was now still in his twenties.

And his was a handsome face—strong, sharp features, with a thick crown of virile, coal-black hair. But the awe that struck Smitty as he looked at the image on the television screen—though long familiar as he was with his chief—was caused by the eyes set in the calm, expressionless face. They were eyes so light-gray in color as to seem without any tint at all. Pale, flaming, cold holes. It seemed that you could look far down into those icy pits into a world of gray fog and personal desolation. Desolation of a soul seared by the treacherous machinations of crime, the underworld which Dick Benson had dedicated his life to smashing in order that other innocent persons might not be similarly injured.

"Yes, Smitty?" came The Avenger's vibrant, compelling voice.

"Something big, chief," said Smitty. "Something so big, and so impossible, that I can hardly believe it happened. A general electric-power failure, lasting, as far as I can judge, from fifteen to twenty seconds."

"How general, Smitty?" came the calm, cool voice.

"I mean *general*!" said Smitty excitedly. "It seems as if every power unit on the North American continent—I didn't take time to try South America—failed for the short length of time I mentioned. *Every* unit! Not just the regular power plants, but ignition systems of cars, boats, everything. It's incredible, chief!"

The pale eyes were taking on a glitter that made them resemble twin diamond drills.

"I happened to be in a place where power failure would not show up, Smitty. So I didn't observe the phenomenon you describe. But if it was as you say, then it is incredible indeed. And rather horrible in its implications. You and Josh and Mac had better hurry to Bleek Street."

Mac hastened to the giant's side. Having listened to the first of the giant's words, he had gone to the phone booth, then hurried back.

"I put a call through to the Newark Airport," he said. "Two planes landed in the last fifteen minutes and reported their ignition systems had gone dead, too."

Which seemed to make it unanimous.

Impossible as it appeared, apparently every electrical unit in North America—in the air, on the ground, on the waters—had gone completely dead for about twenty seconds!

CHAPTER III

A Messenger Dies

The man kept his head down so that his hat brim hid his face and, particularly, his eyes. He was nearly out of his mind with terror. Nearly—but retaining just enough sanity to know that it must show in his face.

Anyone looking into his appalled eyes and seeing the twitching, distorted mask of his face would have reported him at once to the police. And the cops would have detained him for questioning, to see what on earth was the matter.

He didn't dare be detained. He had to get on to New York to a certain address on Bleek Street. Over this address, he had been told, was a small sign with the simple legend, Justice, Inc., lettered on it.

Justice, Inc., where a man called The Avenger helped those who were in dreadful danger, or who were the possessors of such horrible secrets that the regular police could not safeguard them.

This man had to see The Avenger and tell him a

colossal thing. And he didn't know if he could manage to stay alive till he got to The Avenger's headquarters.

He had left Cleveland hours ago. At the very outset, he had almost been murdered. A car had raced up beside him at the depot, and from the car's windows had poured a well-directed hailstorm of bullets.

The man had fallen to the walk and rolled behind a parked car, then crouched and leaped to the next, as slugs battered through the body of the first in deadly search of him.

He had fled to the New York train, scrambled aboard the last car as the train was pulling out—and immediately been grabbed by the arm and yanked into a compartment. A pair of masked men, there, had held guns on him and had said not one word. But the situation was plain enough. As soon as the train rolled clear of the city's outskirts, the two were going to shoot him and throw him off.

The man could scarcely tell, himself, how he had gotten out of that trap. He wouldn't have even tried if the urgency of his message to The Avenger hadn't been so terrific.

There was a confused memory picture of a lunge toward one of the men, two instant shots at him, a searing pain in his right shoulder, and then a picture of one of the two men falling, drilled in the head by his own pal.

He had then slugged the other man and left the compartment.

At Harmon, the man had slid from the train and gone to the nearest freight platform. There were two trucks. He had waited till one pulled away, then had climbed into the cab of the second with a gun in his hand.

"New York, fella, and don't ask questions!"

The driver had taken one look at the dreadful, white face and the terrorized, desperate eyes—and started for New York. The drive down the state had been without incident.

But there, the man knew, the peacefulness was going to end.

They wanted to kill him before he could get to The Avenger.

Who "they" were, he did not know. But he knew why they didn't dare let him get to Bleek Street alive. It was because of what he knew, because of the strange thing on which he, as an expert electrician, had stumbled at Plant 4 near Marville, Ohio.

A mad, tremendous, world-shaking thing!

"They" had lost track of him when he escaped the trap on the train and came on to New York by truck. But they would have a guard posted near his destination. For they knew where he was bound for.

The chances of his getting to Bleek Street, and to the door under that small but mighty sign, Justice, Inc., were very, very slim.

But he *had* to do it.

It was late afternoon when he got within a block of Bleek Street. He debated waiting till night but decided against it. The street lights would pick him out almost as much as daylight. No, he might as well try it now.

The man, as he thought this over, was careful to stay in the heart of an after-work crowd streaming down the sidewalk from their various places of employment. In crowds lies safety, he thought. So he went down the walk with people elbowing him in every direction, like a piece of driftwood on the current of a stream, approaching the corner of Bleek Street.

There, he didn't know quite what he should do.

There was a crowd on this avenue. There would be none on Bleek Street, from what he had heard of the place.

Bleek Street, where Dick Benson had his headquarters, was a quiet little back bay in the midst of lower Manhattan's roaring activity. It was only a block long. One side of the block was taken up by the back of a tremendous concrete warehouse, fronting on the next street.

In the center of the other side were three old red-brick buildings that had been thrown into one. To right and left of the three buildings were empty loft, store, and small warehouse structures all owned or under long lease by The Avenger.

In effect, Richard Benson owned the block. And no one ever went in there save people wanting to see him, which meant that few people would be around. No crowds to shield a man, there.

The Marville electrician bit his lip as he neared the corner. Somebody bumped his right arm violently.

"Sorry," he mumbled, wincing, keeping his head down. That arm had only just ceased oozing blood from the deep groove cut in it by the bullet at Cleveland.

He reached the corner. Bare walk stretched from the crowded avenue to the center entrance, seeming as vast in extent, and as desolate, as the Sahara. He groaned. How could he ever traverse that distance? There'd be guns in every doorway, probably.

He clenched his hands. A sort of moan came from his lips. Then, wildly, blindly, he began to run toward his goal.

He ran like a crazy man, zigzagging, now in the center of the empty street, now on the right-hand side, now on the left, as he strove to put as great a distance as possible between himself and doorways.

He hadn't gone a hundred yards before he realized, with a stifled scream, that it was too late for him to escape his fate!

There would be no bullets. No one would try to kill him now. That was because it wasn't necessary any more.

That hard jostling in the crowd back there, when someone unseen had bumped into his right side. The man's right arm was aching like fire now, with more than the bullet wound. But even as the fiery pain became apparent, it faded, and the arm went numb.

His legs started to go numb, too. Face dreadful, death in his eyes, he staggered on toward the doorway of Justice, Inc.

The top floors of the deceptive-looking three buildings on Bleek Street had been thrown into one tremendous room. Up here was the heart of The Avenger's headquarters. It was to this place that Dick Benson had called Mac and Smitty and Josh.

The three were in there now. In fact, all but one of the small band of indomitable crime fighters were there.

Cole Wilson, another member of Justice, Inc., and the little band's newest member, was not present. An engineer, whose genius in mechanical fields was comparable to the very best in the country, Cole had been called to Washington as a technical adviser on one of the nation's great defense projects. Such were the superlative abilities of The Avenger's aides that their advice was sought freely, and given willingly, in these times of stress when the country's welfare depended on keen minds and exceptional experience.

Blond Nellie Gray, slender, small, demure, sat next to the giant, Smitty. Mac, sandy ropes of eyebrows raised high over his bleak blue eyes, was next to Nellie.

Opposite them sat Josh Newton and his pretty wife, Rosabel. Rosabel had graduated from Tuskegee, too. The two of them were devoted and were seldom far apart.

Behind a big, flat-topped desk was the leader of this little crew whom the underworld feared more than all the police forces of all the land put together, Dick Benson, The Avenger.

He was talking, of course, of that mysterious power blackout that had occurred earlier in the day. And as he talked, the five listened with respect, none more respectfully than Smitty, who, as a fine electrical engineer, recognized his master in The Avenger.

"It seemed to me to be impossible that the queer electrical failure could be due to any natural cause," came The Avenger's calm, cold voice. "That was indicated by the fact that Smitty contacted a liner a hundred miles or so from shore, and found it had had no electrical failure. I got in touch with Europe, China, and South America; those places experienced no such phenomenon. Only this, the North American, continent was affected. And if a natural occurrence were responsible, it is reasonable to suppose that the entire earth would have been affected, not just one corner of the globe. But to make sure, I called meteorological stations and observatories in many sections. There has been no instance on recent record of cosmic disturbance or of electrical storms on a large scale till *after* the blackout."

"So?" said Smitty softly, after a pause.

"So it is pretty conclusive that this thing was done artificially. The blackout of power over our continent was caused by some one man or group of men."

Smitty got to his feet, stammering in his excitement.

"That isn't possible! How on earth could any man blank out all electrical units over such an area? Or even stop any one unit at a distance? There have been rumors of rays that would cause ignition systems—on planes or tanks—to go dead at a distance of several miles. War weapons. But I for one have never believed in its possibility."

"If ye don't believe in a thing," said Mac sarcastically, "then that thing canna happen. Nice, clear reasonin', ye mountain of brawn. But in spite of your beautifully clear logic, *somethin'* made every electrical appliance in North America useless for fifteen or twenty seconds!"

Smitty glared at the Scot and sat down. There was no answer to that. Something *had*!

"What beats me," said Josh thoughtfully, "is that so little has come out in the newspapers."

Nellie shook her sleek blond head.

"It's not so surprising, Josh. Probably every power plant thought it was the only one that failed. And every driver thought it was only his car that went dead for a few seconds. There have been a few humorous stories in various papers, where people got together and thought it was mildly curious that more than one motor should fail at the same time. But that's all."

"The War Department doesn't think it's humorous," observed Smitty.

And that was true enough.

The War Department was running around in circles down in Washington. They had phoned Dick Benson, who was on record as having done several priceless things for the government, a very short time after the power blackout, asking if he would investigate the phenomenon at once. So Benson would have been in on the case even if his own intellectual curiosity hadn't driven him into it.

"I wonder if it was a war move," mused Rosabel, her intelligent dark eyes softly brilliant. "A preliminary, threatening gesture, with a demand from some warlike nation soon to follow."

"What I'm wondering," said Smitty, "is not what it was done for, but *how* it was done. It's simply impossible, I tell you. The power plants I contacted didn't report any breakdowns. Their generators were turning, driven either by water power or steam. Only, for a little while, power ceased to be generated. It . . . it's—"

What it was, he was never to be allowed to say. For at that moment there was a tiny pinpoint of red light in a section of wall near the door.

Mac went to a miniature television set designed by Smitty. Always on, it showed anyone entering the vestibule downstairs.

Mac gazed at the screen now, and exclaimed aloud.

"There's a mon at the buzzer. He seems sick—down on his knees—*Whoosh*! He's in a bad way. Smitty!"

But the giant was way ahead of him. He was already out the door and down the stairs. In the vestibule, he gathered a moaning, almost senseless form in his arms, and he raced back up the stairs with it as if his burden had weighed no more than a doll.

He laid the man gently on a divan, with the rest gathering around.

Dick Benson took over. His pale eyes, like stainless steel chips, stared compellingly into the man's blurring ones.

"You wanted to see me?"

The man's lips moved, but no sound came out. He nodded a very little.

"What did you want to see me about?"

Nellie's eyes were sympathetic. From the fact that The Avenger, one of the world's greatest physicians, was making no effort to aid the man, she knew that such effort was hopeless, that the fellow must be dying, with nothing on earth able to stay his fate.

The man was unable to answer the question. His eyes closed, but with a last flicker of desperate strength, he struggled to an elbow.

"Midnight, April 27th—" he gasped.

He fell back. And they knew there was nothing more to do with him, except bury him.

Dick's hands, slim and not large, but steely in their strength, went over the man's body. They paused at the right arm, and his icily flaring eyes glared at a small red spot.

"Poisoned!" he said. "Hypodermic needle. Murdered to keep from telling what he came here to tell."

CHAPTER IV

The Rooted Needles

Janet Weems's hair was a light brown and streaked with dark gold as if the sun had been at it. She had deep-brown eyes and a smooth, satiny skin. She was a little taller than most girls, and much more graceful. The man, looking at her, found her just about perfect.

But, then, he would have found her about perfect even if she hadn't actually come so close to it, for he was in love with her.

The man was Bill Burton, newly in charge of Marville's Plant 4, and Janet Weems was his secretary, soon to become his wife.

Burton looked haggard and ten years older than his real age, which was natural enough. For nearly two months, he had been frantically investigating a generating plant that wouldn't work, but which, to the trained eye, was absolutely unsurpassed in design and execution.

Bill Burton and Janet Weems were not in Marville now. They were in Cleveland. And they were hiding in

Cleveland, under assumed names, as if they were wanted by the whole police force for murder.

This was because at last Burton, who was an extra-competent engineer, had found something at Marville. Something half explaining the failure of perfectly wired, perfectly installed, swiftly turning generators to generate power as they were supposed to do.

Something that had kept him from sleeping or eating ever since. Something that had sent him at once to Cleveland, after taking elaborate precautions to make sure he was not trailed. He meant to board a plane for New York, now.

But not with Janet.

He knew his life wasn't worth a plugged nickel and refused to have her share peril with him any more than was necessary. Even if she traveled alone, it was going to be dangerous enough.

"The name," he said tensely, "is Richard Henry Benson. Have you got that?"

"Richard Henry Benson," repeated Janet. Her lips were pale with worry over Bill. He was so obviously beside himself with fear, terrorized by something he had found at Marville.

"Benson is the one sometimes called The Avenger," Burton added.

"Rather a melodramatic name," said Janet, frowning a little.

"He doesn't call himself that. I have an idea he doesn't care for it much. Others, particularly crooks, who are afraid of him, have tacked on the label. But no matter. You are to go to this Richard Henry Benson, at Bleek Street in New York. Any cab-driver will know the address instantly, and there is only one tenanted entrance on the street, as I understand it, so you can't miss."

"Benson, Bleek Street," nodded Janet. "And when I get there, what do I say?"

Burton hesitated a long time. What he had in mind

was too appalling to tell even Janet. He shrank from doing so. He had an unreasonable feeling that just the knowledge, in her brain, would be dangerous to her.

Finally he reached into his pocket and drew out a small envelope. From the envelope he took two slim lengths of steel, pointed at the ends like needles. At the blunt end of each needle he had taped a very fine strand of copper wire.

They looked like needles with roots on them.

From another pocket he took a diagram. The diagram was simple. It represented one of the needles—whether big or little could not be told since there was nothing else in the drawing for comparison of size—standing upright on a wavy line. The needle's "root" went down under this wavy line, and from the needle's tip went up a flock of other lines, straight lines, none of which quite touched the point.

He folded the diagram so that it would be encompassed in the envelope and slid the needles back in also.

"Give him this," he said, sealing the envelope.

"Bill—what do they mean?"

Burton said nothing.

"Darling, what did you find out at the plant? It must have been just in the last day or two. Before that time you were worried, but that was all. Since then you have been more than worried. You have been afraid—terribly afraid!"

Burton only shook his head. He had a firm chin, anyhow. It was stubborn as granite now. And his lips were a thin straight line in his face.

"You won't tell me?"

"No, honey, I won't," he said. "Time for us to get going. I'll go out first. You follow in a few minutes. One of us must get through to Benson. You understand? One of us *must* get through!"

"Oh, Bill!"

Janet's arms were around his neck, and she was kissing

33

him. Then he went out, shoulders back, like a soldier going over the top to a war adventure from which he knew he would never return.

Janet had taken a room in a small, side-street hotel, where Bill had met her. He went out the door with his head down and hurried up the block and around the corner. His car was parked there.

For a full minute he stood in a doorway near the corner and looked around. He was trying to see if anyone was lurking near his machine. He had to wait till several people on the walk went on their way, to be sure they were the innocent pedestrians they seemed to be.

Because of the delay, Janet saw the thing that ensued just a little later.

She gave Burton four minutes, then left the room herself.

In her effort to keep her movements secret, she did not formally check out of the hotel. She left money to cover her bill on the dresser, with a note. In the small lobby, she walked past the desk with only a nod to the clerk, as if she were merely going out for dinner somewhere.

She, too, went out of the entrance as unobtrusively as possible, and her way lay up the block, in the wake of Burton's steps, toward a taxi stand in the next square.

She reached the corner, glanced down, and saw Burton's car. She could see the back of his head, through the rear window of the coupé, as he settled behind the wheel.

Her heart was in that look. Dear Bill, so afraid of something. And it was so unlike him to be afraid of anything—

She heard a scream rip out in the rumble of traffic sounds, then another, and another. But after the first high, awful cry, the screams sounded only in her own ears. And they sounded so because they were her own.

No one else heard them because a roar of noise drowned every other sound on the street.

She had seen Bill's body move a little, as if he had put his foot on the starter. Then there had been blue flame a full story high, blossoming from the car! And, after that, no more car.

Where the car had been, was a solid, mushrooming pall of black smoke!

The roar of the explosion boomed down the canyon of the street. There was a clang as the hood of the car fell half a block away.

Then Janet heard her own screams again. But only for a few seconds. Nerves can only stand such a shock for a few seconds.

Her screams died out as if she had been throttled; then, with her horrified eyes wide on that ugly smoke-growth that had been a car, she sagged to the sidewalk with blackness closing in on her . . .

"Easy does it, now. She just fainted, that's all. At first I thought she'd been hit by a piece of metal or something when that car blew up. But she's all right—"

Janet's fluttering eyelids opened. She looked dazedly around.

She saw bottles and boxes and hot-water bags and cigarettes. She was in a drugstore. Towering over her was a good-natured-looking cop. But in his kindly face was a grim look, too, aftermath of the explosion.

"Coming around, huh, miss?" he said. "We carried you here to this store thinking we'd send for a doctor. But you don't seem to need one. I'll phone right away, though, if you'd like—"

"I don't need a doctor," Janet said.

Her voice was hoarse, tremulous. She was surprised, however, that she could talk at all.

"Any place you'd like to be taken, miss?"

Janet was incapable of thought. She was still seeing

Bill's car, with Bill in it, blown to bits when he pressed the starter. But, by a sort of instinct, she said the right thing.

She was supposed to go somewhere with something, at once, even though tragedy had just blasted her life.

Needles with roots. A diagram.

"No, I'm perfectly all right," she heard herself say. "I'll get a cab—"

"I'll get one for you."

The cop helped her out of the store. Leaning heavily on his arm, she went to the cab he summoned with his police whistle. She got in.

Only then did she think to look for the envelope Burton had given her.

Her handbag was gone, of course. But that didn't matter. She had a few large bills in her stocking top, and the priceless envelope—at least, Bill had acted as if it were priceless—had been thrust into the bosom of her dress.

Her hand felt blindly, numbly, for it.

The envelope wasn't there!

No telling how long she had lain on the sidewalk, with curious bystanders around her, before that policeman had carried her to the drugstore. No telling who had been among the bystanders.

But one thing was definite enough. The envelope with the rooted needles and the diagram had been stolen!

Janet Weems's brain cracked definitely at that. She thought she fainted again. Anyway, a curtain seemed to descend over her senses.

She didn't know that she got out of the cab at the airport, looking almost normal, and paid the driver. She didn't know that she walked almost steadily into the airport's administration building, bought a ticket for New York, and boarded a plane.

She knew none of these things, for her subconscious brain was taking over and urging her on the path that had been impressed upon her just before tragedy struck. Her conscious brain was off some place, treading the thin line between sanity and madness.

CHAPTER V

Death Out Of Marville

The buzzer made a discreet sound. The light winked over Telephone 6 on The Avenger's desk.

There was no such thing as a jangling phone bell in this sanctum of the world's most unique crime-fighter. There was a soft buzzer to draw attention, and then a light to show which telephone was being rung. For Dick Benson had a battery of phones on his desk that would almost have made the phones in a broker's office look scant.

Benson picked the instrument up in slim, white, steel-strong fingers.

"Yes?" he said.

"General Hospital calling Mr. Benson," a voice sounded over the wire.

The Avenger's cold, pale eyes took on a look of glacier ice under a midnight sun.

It was said of Benson that he had no fear. And that

was probably true in a personal fashion. But it was not true that he was without *all* fear.

Dick feared for his associates' safety. He always carried this fear with him. The courageous little band ran such terrible risks at all times that Dick was constantly fearing to pick up a phone and hear just this sort of thing: "So-and-so Hospital calling. There is a Mr. Smith here—" Or MacMurdie or Josh or Rosabel or Nellie—

But this was not that dreaded occasion.

"There is a girl here by the name of Janet Weems, as far as we can tell from an engraved pin, who wants to speak to Mr. Benson."

"Benson talking," said The Avenger. "Put her on the wire."

"I'm afraid that is impossible, sir," came the voice. "Miss Weems is very ill. I'm afraid you will have to come here."

"What does she want to see me about?"

There was a hesitation. Then the voice said, "We really don't know. Miss Weems is delirious. But over and over she calls your name. Dr. Daggit, of our staff, said to phone and ask if you would come; he believes Miss Weems might be helped by your visit."

"I'll be over at once, of course," said Benson quietly.

He hung up, and turned to the big cabinet containing a twin to the marvelous television set in Mac's drugstore.

"Smitty! Benson calling. Smitty! Smitty—"

In about six seconds the giant's voice sounded over his belt radio. This was a two-way set so small that it could be worn unnoticed at the waist in a thin, form-fitting metal case no larger than a cigar case. Smitty was the designer of this, too, and all the little crew wore them.

"Right, chief," rumbled the giant.

"Smitty, meet me at General Hospital, at once."

Smitty pulled up at the broad entrance of the hospital

a minute after The Avenger got there. They went in and were shown to the office of Dr. Daggit.

Daggit, a thin, serious-looking man with a surgeon's hands and a brain doctor's sardonic eye, shook his head when Miss Weems's name was mentioned.

"I hesitated whether to call you or not," he admitted. "The girl is completely irrational. I doubt very much whether she will have anything coherent to tell you when you do see her. Yet, as you were told over the phone, she is so desperately anxious to talk to you that we thought a visit might help her."

"Is there any clue at all to what she wishes to see me about?" asked Benson.

Daggit shrugged.

"She keeps talking about an envelope. She never describes it; doesn't say what's in it. There is simply, it seems, an envelope."

"Was an envelope found in her personal possessions?"

Daggit stared curiously, and with a little inward shiver, at the appalling, colorless eyes of this man whom he knew not alone as a crime fighter, but also as a brain specialist far superior to himself.

"She had no personal possessions," he said. "Not even a handbag. Certainly no envelope."

"Let's have a talk with her," said Dick.

They went to a room, Smitty hulking gigantic in The Avenger's wake, Daggit leading the way.

"She's pretty," said Smitty, looking down at the girl who stared back, vacant-eyed, from the bed. "And she must have had an awful bad knock recently," he added, looking at her tapering fingers, which picked aimlessly at a covering sheet.

"Miss Weems," said The Avenger, voice compelling, vibrant.

The vacant, deep-brown eyes turned toward him. His pale eyes stared down.

"I am Richard Benson. You wanted to see me."

Almost, for an instant, there was a glint of reason in the blank, beautiful eyes. But then they wandered again, and the trembling fingers worried the sheet.

"Needles," she said.

Daggit looked at Benson.

"I don't know what that means," he whispered. "But she hasn't mentioned needles before—"

"Needles," came her voice. "Needles with roots. In the envelope."

"What about the needles?" Dick said, his voice hypnotic. But there is no hypnosis of a person without a will of his own.

"In the envelope. A diagram. Needles with roots. Have to get through to Benson. Must see Benson. What will I tell him, Bill?" She screamed. "It exploded! It exploded. He's dead!"

"You must get through to Benson," The Avenger repeated. "Yes. That's right. And when you see him you are to tell him—what?"

But it was over. She wasn't going to talk any more.

She turned her pretty face away, and her hands were stilled.

The Avenger straightened up.

"I think she'll come out of this pretty soon," he said to Dr. Daggit. "I defer to your more thorough examination, of course. But it seems to me there is no indication of brain fever or anything with lasting effects. Simply amnesia resulting from a great shock—"

There was a heavy clanging sound from the door.

"Good heavens!" exclaimed Daggit.

The Avenger said nothing. He moved, quick as fluid light, toward the one window of the room. No need to tell Benson what had happened; he knew.

General Hospital is equipped to handle mental cases.

Janet Weems, brought into the place either delirious or more permanently mentally deranged, had been taken to a room equipped to take care of violent patients.

It was equipped with a solid metal door outside the regular wooden one, which could be slid closed if necessary.

That outer metal door had just been banged shut. Hard!

Daggit's exclamation had been one of sheer surprise, not of apprehension. But The Avenger had leaped for the window because he was much more than surprised. He knew that the closing of the door could not have been an accident. It must have been deliberate. But the window—

He had almost reached it when there was a snap here, too, and from a slot in the sill a metal plate covered the glass pane.

The metal was to keep raving maniacs from breaking the glass and injuring themselves, just as the metal door was to keep them from breaking out and injuring others.

But the steel of the barriers made no distinctions. Sane or insane, anyone in the room would be hopelessly kept in that room when the plates banged shut.

Daggit grabbed for the room phone. "Operator. Operator!"

The line was dead. The wire had been cut just outside the wall somewhere.

"I . . . I seem to have trouble in breathing—" Daggit said.

Dick Benson had noted the difficulty a few seconds before the doctor. Gas had been let into this room, from some opening, with the closing of door and window.

They were caught in a trap, to die of gas, unless—

"Smitty!" said Benson.

He didn't say any more. He nodded his black-cropped head toward the window, and the giant went to it, picking up a chair as he moved.

Benson took a handkerchief from his pocket and went to the bed. He pressed it over the nostrils and mouth of the girl there, who made no protest but only looked at him with blank, grave eyes.

Smitty, noticing, took out his own handkerchief and tossed it to Daggit.

Gas was a much-used weapon in the fight of the underworld against The Avenger and his crew, so each of them went always prepared. Each kept a coat lapel saturated with a chemical of MacMurdie's invention that would nullify the effects of gas and, in addition, carried at least one handkerchief similarly saturated.

But the chemical could only stall off the effects of a lethal gas for a short time before becoming useless, and it looked as if they would be in that room a very long time before breaking out.

"You can't batter that steel down," said Daggit to Smitty. "It was designed to withstand just such assaults."

Smitty said nothing. He raised the chair. It was of metal and very strong.

"Big as you are—" began Daggit, pessimistically.

The chair fairly whistled through the air as Smitty's vast arms swung it.

It hit against the metal shield like a steam hammer on a boiler plate.

And nothing seemed to happen.

"I told you," said Daggit. "Good heavens! Who could have done such a thing? Right in the hospital! This is chlorine gas—deadly! And we can't get out—"

"You had better," said The Avenger calmly, "save your breath and inhale through the handkerchief."

Bang!

The ponderous metal chair slammed against the steel curtain again. The chair, with the two blows, was beginning to take on the shape of a pretzel.

Smitty was gasping. He was unable to breathe through his lapel properly and still swing the chair. But he saw, if no one else did, that the steel curtain was giving a very little in the center.

Bang!

Dr. Daggit's eyes were wide. Never before had he seen such a blow. And he didn't think he ever would again. Under it, the two metal chair legs bent clear around on themselves.

And the steel shield bellied inward in the middle like the bottom of a dishpan with a hundred-pound rock dropped on it from a second-story window.

Bang!

"That does it," said Smitty, tottering a little with the deadly effects of the gas.

He whipped his lapel over his nose with his left hand, and got his right into the crack, between steel and window frame, resulting from the bending of the metal.

He braced his feet against the wall, and with shoulders, legs, and enormous right hand, he pulled.

The shield bent back into the room like the top of a tin can bent over after it has been two-thirds cut with a can-opener.

Smitty smashed the glass of the window, and the gas began swirling out. Daggit stared at the big man with eyes that were still wide with wonder.

"It isn't possible," he said. "These metal sheets were designed against just such efforts by strong men. And you could do *that* to one of them! I sincerely hope you are never brought into this place as a patient, my friend."

Smitty grinned. They waited till the head nurse, on her regular round, came to the door and rectified the "mistake" someone had made in shutting the steel door on a staff doctor and a couple of visitors.

By then it was much too late to get hold of the killer who had tried to murder them all in the room where Janet Weems lay. So Benson didn't even try.

While waiting for the door to be opened—*that* panel was a bit too massive even for Smitty—Benson had gone over the girl's clothing. And he had seen a dress label that instantly caught his attention.

The label proclaimed that the frock had been bought in a store in an Ohio town called Marville. And it had brought the diamond glitter instantly to The Avenger's pale, icy eyes because this was the second time the name of that town had cropped up recently.

He had partially traced the man who had died at Bleek Street after getting out the strangled words: "Midnight, April 27—" Traced him to Cleveland, then to Marville, Ohio. And he had tentatively fixed the man's occupation as that of electrician because of tiny fragments of rubber in the welt of his shoe sole, identifiable as the type used in electric-cable insulation, and because of microscopic bits of copper under his fingernails.

A man racing against death to Bleek Street from Marville, Ohio! Now, a girl coming from the same place, having skirted danger so terrible that it had temporarily deranged her mind, but who was still mumbling that she "must get through to Benson!"

"Get Mac, Smitty," Dick said to the giant. "Meet me at the hangar. We're taking a plane to Marville."

CHAPTER VI

Plant 4

By desperate efforts, Grant Utilities had managed to keep the light of publicity off the fantastic failure of their new Plant 4. The papers hadn't printed the story. But you didn't have to be in Marville long before you heard about it.

And a man like Dick Benson didn't have to hear about such a bizarre thing twice before he was instantly on his way to investigate. About twenty-five minutes after landing in Marville's small airport, Benson and Mac and Smitty drew up in a rented car before the entrance of the useless power plant.

They were about two miles from Marville, in a section that, with the shallow gorge in Marville River which made the rapids powering the turbines, was too craggy and wild for other structures. No one lived near the plant; the countryside was very quiet.

"Feels kind of creepy around here," was Smitty's reaction to the unusual silence and desolation.

They went in. Benson asked to see the engineer in charge.

The man he questioned was a big fellow in dungarees with a dark and sullen face.

"You mean Bill Burton? He ain't here."

"Where is he?"

"Don't know. He went to Cleveland, and I ain't heard from him since."

"Then," said Benson, pale eyes fixed on the darkly sullen face, "I'll ask my questions of you."

"I'm not answerin' any questions," the man snapped. "So you can go roll your hoop some place else."

When any person, great or humble, refused to answer The Avenger's questions in that half-frightened, half-defiant tone, in spite of the glacial compulsion of the cold, pale eyes, there was something wrong.

Smitty got the retreating man in one leap. The giant held him off the floor with his great left hand clutching a fold of the denim jacket at the man's neck. It was like holding up a kitten by the nape of the neck.

Smitty's vast right, doubled into an unbelievable fist, gently touched the man's jaw at the end of a two-inch stab. The fellow's head rocked.

"You've been asked a civil question," Smitty said silkily. "You'll be asked a few more. We sincerely hope you'll be good enough to answer them all."

The man's frightened eyes showed that he had decided to be very good indeed, and when he was released, he answered questions promptly.

The incredible tale came out.

A fine, modern power plant with generators, turned by the turbines, whining their swift song. The latest in plant design, all checked many times for errors.

And no power coming from it.

Smitty's first doubled again.

"You're lying," he rumbled. "That isn't possible."

"It's the truth," said the man quickly. "I swear it!

There was a dedication, see? The Marville mayor threw the main switch to start things things off. And nothing happened. No power, see? But everything seemed all right. And still does."

The Avenger's eyes were flaring bits of bright ice. And Smitty's fist slowly uncoiled as he recalled that about the same story had lain in the recent brief power failure in New York.

Whirring generators, nothing perceptibly wrong, and no power being generated.

"All right," he growled, "what's the answer?"

"We don't know," said the man, looking at the giant's great hands. "But I think it's got something to do with Nevlo."

"Nevlo?" said The Avenger, voice as icy as his eyes.

"He was chief engineer here before Burton. He laid out the joint, and then he got fired. Bad-tempered guy with black hair and eyes; held his head to the left all the time."

"How could he keep the plant from functioning?"

"How do I know?" snarled the man. He changed tone and expression as the great fists began to double again. "I mean, nobody knows," he said. "All we know is that Nevlo laughed when the dedication went sour, and he swore the plant would never be any good till he was back running it again."

Smitty and The Avenger looked at each other. The thought behind the china-blue eyes of the giant, and the dread pale eyes of Benson was the same:

Possibly a man could do such a thing. If so, it would be only another step from stopping one power plant to stopping all power plants.

"But a mon would have to be a wizard—" began MacMurdie. Then he stopped, and all listened.

Outside, on the graveled road ending at the plant's entrance, came the sound of a rapidly driven car. An old car, judging by the rattles. They looked out a lofty window and saw an ancient flivver shudder to a stop. A man in a cheap gray suit, with a cap on, raced from the car and into the plant.

"Pete!" he yelled to the man with the dark face. He paid no attention to the others. "Pete, I just saw Nevlo!"

"Nevlo?" barked the other man. "You sure? Everybody in the company's been trying to find him. Are you *sure*?"

"Yeah, I'm sure. You can't mistake the guy—tall, black-haired, with his head held over to the left. Sure, it was Nevlo. But he won't look like that any more!"

The Avenger caught the man's shoulder. He didn't mean to hurt him, but such was the power of his slim white hands that the man screamed a little with what Benson meant to be only a firm pressure.

It was the second man's turn to get the full shock of staring into the pale clarity of Benson's eyes. He shivered and stood still, even though the slim, steely fingers were compressing his flesh to the bone.

"What do you mean Nevlo won't look like that any more?" Benson demanded.

"It's like this," whimpered the man. "I see Nevlo off on the top of a mound across the gorge from the plant. There's a little bare spot on the mound, with trees around, and he's in the bare spot. He's standing beside something that sticks up from the ground like a radio antenna. I start to go closer to him because I want to tell him that Blake, president of the company, wants to see him. Any of us who find Nevlo are to do that. But before I get near enough there's a hell of a big blue flash from the thing like an antenna, so big it blinds me and I don't see anything but electric blue for a second. When I look again, I see Nevlo running from the place where the antenna was. But there's nothing there any more. There's just a blue hole in the ground. And Nevlo ain't the same. He's running like a gorilla, with half his clothes burned off, and he's yelling like a crazy man."

"You think the explosion, or whatever it was, did that to him?" said Benson.

"Yeah! I think the accident crippled him some way and drove him nuts. I think he was experimenting with something, and it went wrong."

There was silence, in which the dark-faced Pete forgot to be sulky, and Benson's face was calmly pensive, and Mac and Smitty stared in something like horror at each other.

A man capable, in some grimly miraculous way, of stopping a power plant—perhaps of stopping all power plants! And now—if this fellow's story was true—a man warped in body and soul by some experimental slip! A madman!

Benson sped toward the exit, with Mac and Smitty after him.

Blake, president of Grant Utilities Corp., was in Cleveland most of the time at the general office. But he had been in the smaller Marville offices a great deal lately, while the best electrical brains in the country tried to straighten out Plant 4.

He was there now, and in residence at his Marville estate. And he saw Benson in a hurry when that rather mythical name was sent in to his private office.

"I have heard of you as a great electrical engineer," he said. It was a common greeting. Doctors had heard of Richard Benson as a great physician; financiers as a wizard promoter; lawyers as a master of law. For The Avenger was profoundly skilled in more professions and activities, perhaps, than any other man on earth.

"More recently," said Blake, "I've heard of you as an investigator. And now you are in Marville." He gnawed at his lower lip a moment, making no effort to mask the fact that he was agitated by the visit. "You have been out to Plant 4?"

"Yes," nodded Dick, his pale eyes taking the measure of the big, sleek man who headed Grant Utilities Corp. A worried man. A harassed man. A *frightened* man! Fear rode in his eyes and underlay his outwardly composed manner.

Blake wasted no time in stalling.

"If you've been out to the plant, I suppose you know of the trouble there."

Benson nodded.

"The men have strict orders not to talk—" began Blake.

"It was necessary that they do so," said Benson, "so they did. I understand your present chief engineer is a man named William Burton. Is that right?"

"Yes, that's correct."

"Where is he now?"

The fear showed more plainly.

"I . . . I don't know."

"Is the name Janet Weems familiar to you, Mr. Blake?"

Blake jumped a little. "Why, yes. She is Burton's secretary. That is, part of the time she helps him make out his reports, and the rest of the time she is in the Marville office. She . . . hasn't been around lately, either."

"Nor your former engineer, Nevlo?"

"Nor Nevlo," said Blake. And then he began to swear, though he didn't look like a man who was often profane. "Nevlo, damn him! He's responsible for the failure of Plant 4. For a long time I didn't believe it. I couldn't believe that a man could stop a power plant. But I believe it now. I'm beginning to be convinced that no power on earth can get Plant 4 running again if Nevlo doesn't want it to."

"How could he keep it from working?"

"I don't know," said the unhappy Blake. He spread his hands. "I'm in a bad spot, Mr. Benson. I don't mind admitting it. I'm president of this corporation, but I'm answerable to the stockholders. And they're beginning to ride the daylights out of me because Plant 4 doesn't begin operations. And the directors—" He shrugged helplessly.

"I can understand how it might take some explaining," said Benson quietly. "And you have no idea where Burton or Miss Weems can be reached?"

Blake said nothing. He was staring over the Avenger's shoulder at something.

Blake's desk was placed so that, if he looked a little to the left, he saw a corner window. He was looking there now, rigid, eyes unblinking.

"You don't know where Burton and the girl are?" The Avenger repeated.

Still Blake said nothing. And now his eyes began to take on a glazed look from sheer horror. A sort of croak came from his distorted lips, and he tried to point.

Mac and Smitty and Benson whirled toward the window.

"*Whoosh!*" exclaimed Mac in a suffocated tone.

"For—" gasped Smitty.

Benson said nothing. He jumped for the window.

Out there, hanging onto no visible support at all, as far as could be seen, was a sort of mad gorilla form. A man, yet with the face of an insane beast, dressed in clothes that were burned and torn till they were little more than rags.

"*Nevlo!*" panted Blake.

The hideous face disappeared. Benson got the window up and looked down.

Blake's office was on the second floor. Down below, a crooked, distorted gorilla form was just dropping from the serrated bricks of the wall onto the sidewalk.

They saw him knock aside several screaming pedestrians and then disappear around the corner of the building. Smitty and Mac raced for the stairs, but they knew they'd not reach the street in time to see the ape-like figure.

"Nevlo—mad!" whispered Blake.

Benson said nothing. It was not necessary to add words.

A man discharged, formerly just vindictive. Now a lunatic from a misdirected experiment. A madman loose with a tremendous destructive secret in his crazed brain.

A madman with power to shake the world!

CHAPTER VII

The Dead Line

Practically on the threshold of The Avenger's odd Bleek Street headquarters, a man had died. He had died mumbling about the date April 27th, which had been only a few days away at that time.

The man had come from Marville, where a power plant had failed, and he was an electrician. It was obvious that he was connected with that plant. Furthermore, it was a probability that he had discovered something about the nature of that failure and had come running to tell Dick Benson about it. Death had stopped him!

But he had managed to gasp the one statement: "Midnight, April 27th—"

What would happen then? Almost certainly a thing that had occurred before.

Another general power failure, perhaps brief, perhaps permanent.

Of course, all this was deduction, not provable; and

the date might have to do with something else. But it was the most reasonable assumption to be made; so The Avenger was acting on it.

Acting on it in the air.

Patient checking of the power failures during that as yet not much commented on, but grimly significant, interval when nearly all electrical units were useless had revealed a curious thing.

The dead area was in a huge, rough diamond shape on the map that took in most of North America. The diamond shape was bounded vaguely by a line drawn from some point in New England, down toward the equator, up to some point in California, toward Hudson Bay in Canada, then back to New England.

Within that diamond shape, no electrical power. But the few power units outside the diamond—like the ship at sea radioed by Smitty and a few small plants in British Columbia and Alaska—had not been affected.

In one section, no power; outside the section, no trouble.

Benson wanted to know the exact location and slant of any one of those four lines forming the diamond. The two slanting south from New England and north toward Hudson Bay were the nearest at hand. However, the southern line lay out to sea, as far as could be judged. Any plane going dead out there might drown its pilot. So that line was out.

There remained the northern line to investigate.

Now, at a few minutes to midnight, April 27th, all five of Benson's aids and Dick, himself, were up cruising.

There were five planes—Mac, Smitty, Nellie, and Dick piloted one each, and Josh and Rosabel were in the fifth. The five planes had orders to tack back and forth at twenty-mile intervals along the line, as at present located, and search for the demarcation point, on one side of which the ignition systems functioned and on the other side of which they went blank.

The five kept in communication with each other.

"Smitty, chief," the giant's far voice came over the radio. "Four minutes to twelve. Nothing's happened, yet."

Benson nodded a little. Josh's precise tones sounded. "Everything all right so far, Mr. Benson. Three minutes to go."

Nellie reported, then Mac. The minute hand of Dick's watch began to edge onto the midnight hour.

The Avenger banked his plane and started back along the line he had just taken. A line designed to cross at a right angle the vaguely placed line of power failure. And his four other planes performed the same kind of maneuver, up and up toward Hudson Bay, twenty miles apart.

The second hand moved toward the exact second of midnight. Benson, as nearly as he could calculate, was in the diamond, heading toward the area that had not been affected by the last failure. There was no guarantee, of course, that a second failure—if there were a second one—would occur in precisely the same section. But all he had to work on was the last one.

He was in the dead area, as far as he knew. The second hand passed the minute mark, and it was midnight; and his motor thrummed steadily along.

Midnight, and everything was disconcertingly all right.

Benson banked again and began retracing his line. It was possible that he had gone farther northeast, away from the diamond, than he had calculated. He'd go southwest again.

It was a moonless, black night with the stars like white diamonds on blue velvet—clear, but not giving off much light. Beneath The Avenger and ahead were the lights of a town. Not many lights because the village was small, and it was late. But enough to show a town was there.

He passed over it at twenty-five thousand feet, and went on—

His motor went dead!

There was no slow failure, no sputtering around and then catching and then coughing again. *Zing!* The motor shut off as if he had cut the ignition switch.

This was it!

Benson looked behind, pale eyes like ice under a glacial moon. The lights of the village still blazed behind him. But here, not three miles beyond, was the dead area.

He planed slowly downward with a dead motor, wheeling and gliding for the lights. Just as he was about to cross directly above them, his motor caught again.

There it was. The curious line of demarcation with light and life on one side and blackness and power-death on the other. Literally a dead line.

Benson had it now. He spread his map and charted his exact position. Meanwhile he glided lower and lower, back and forth across the line.

It was eerie. The motor went dead, caught again when he retraced his flight, went dead on the return. It was as if he passed through an invisible wall and into a spot where other-world conditions prevailed, and electricity, among other commonplace phenomena, did not function.

During a "live" period he tried to raise the others on the radio. There was no answer from any of the other four planes. It looked as if all had been caught in the fatal diamond.

Then, abruptly, his motor caught while he was to the *south* of the line. At the same moment, lights burst out in a formerly black area far ahead on the horizon, as a town that had been plunged in darkness began receiving power again.

The strange blackout was over.

But whereas the first one had only lasted between fifteen and twenty seconds, this one had endured for over eight minutes!

Dick's radio chattered. It was Mac.

"Motor and radio dead for eight minutes, Muster Benson," came the Scot's burring voice. "I had enough altitude to keep in the air with a dead motor. Now, radio and motor okay."

The rest radioed in, too, one by one. All but Dick had been too far within the diamond and had been caught when their ignitions failed.

One by one, The Avenger told them the same thing.

"Meet me at the Portland flying field immediately."

Smitty was the only one whose curiosity caused him to question his chief's orders.

"Portland it is. Heading for it now at three-eighty an hour. But why Portland, chief?"

"Because," said Benson, "the power line, as I charted it, slants down from the north magnetic pole at an angle bringing it directly to or through Portland, Maine."

Dick Benson and his associates knew every landing field in the country, plus a great many emergency landing spots known to few pilots. In a very short time The Avenger's plane nosed down on a long slant toward the distant lights of Portland.

Stars like diamonds on a midnight-blue velvet background. Stars that twinkled in the clear night but gave off very little light. The night was so dark, indeed, that even the pale, infallible eyes of The Avenger didn't see the things for quite a while—till the plane was almost unavoidably upon them.

The first thing he saw was a star, low on the horizon, blink mysteriously out like a light that has been turned off, and then blink on again. After that, he saw a section of night-light design of Portland ahead of him similarly blotted out.

And with that he brought the nose of the plane up in a screaming zoom and gave the motor everything it would take.

His face was calm and expressionless; his eyes were

unwinking in their deadly coldness. Yet, with the brief blinking out of the star and the ground lights, he knew at once what faced him.

Balloons—with, no doubt, net or cable between to catch him. Someone had heard his radio command to the rest to come to Portland airport. Someone had instantly managed to get hold of some test balloon-barrage equipment, with which the army had been experimenting near Portland, and had sent the death trap up into the black night sky. A short notice of that army test with balloons and netting similar to London's aerial defense had been in the papers recently.

Probably no other man could have caught the fleeting hints of the deadly bags so soon in the blackness of a moonless night and could have acted on it so swiftly.

Benson leveled off high above the altitude at which he had barely raked the top of the net. His pale eyes were like agate with cold embers behind them as he debated a calmly considered bout with death.

Mac's plane had been nearest him along the mythical power line. Mac would be in here, on the same side of the field, in a few minutes. And there was that aerial death trap in his way.

By a thousand-to-one chance, he might escape as Benson had. But The Avenger didn't consider thousand-to-one chances on the safety of his aides if he could help it.

He glided down again, watching with eyes like the eyes of a hawk. Now, forewarned, he could get a glimpse of the bags from closer up, outlining them by the stars they eclipsed. There were six of them, three high, three low, spread far apart, making it almost impossible to land on the Portland field from the west. Perhaps more than six—

The Avenger reached for a bracket above the control board. There was a gun there looking at a casual glance much like a standard army rifle. A closer examination would have disclosed a lot of difference, however.

The gun had a smooth bore; was unrifled. It loaded both at muzzle and breech. Into the breech went a powder cartridge without a charge. Into the muzzle went a thing that looked like an apple on a long stick. The stick just fitted the barrel of the gun. The "apple" was an explosive case containing colored powders that gave off skyrocket flares when they were released.

The thing was like a miniature trench mortar, designed for night signaling. But it could do excellent work right now. Work that had nothing to do with sending signals.

Benson swept back along the top line of gas bags. The gun thudded with its extra-heavy recoil against his shoulder. There was a bonfire in the sky, and then there were five balloons.

Six flashing trips back and forth. Six shots. Six aerial fires. And down below, somewhere in the night, was a heap of tangled cable, a trap that had been destroyed before it could destroy.

When Benson landed, wondering field attendants surrounded his plane, puzzled and alarmed by the fires in the sky.

"Captive balloons with cable," Dick explained briefly. "Stolen from the army warehouse, no doubt. They were a menace, so I shot them down. Phone the warehouse; have the loss checked and government operatives set to tracing the thieves."

In the sky could be seen the lights of Mac's plane as it passed serenely through a space that would have caught it in a deadly web if The Avenger hadn't intervened.

"When that plane lands," Benson commanded quietly, "direct the pilot to the administration building. I'll be in the manager's office. There will be three more planes landing in the next half-hour, with the lettering 'Justice,

Inc.,' on their fuselages. Send the occupants to the manager's office, too."

He went off, a gray steel bar of a man, leaving the attendants gaping.

The plane Benson had pointed to came in. A man with the map of Scotland on his homely, freckled face stepped out and was told where to go.

In a short time Benson's five aides were in the manager's office with him. The manager himself, alternately thrilled and alarmed at the presence of a man like Benson, was outside at his stenographer's desk. Benson called him. He ordered a car.

"What's the next stop, Muster Benson, now we're together?" asked MacMurdie.

"The Portland radio station."

Their eyes asked more questions.

"Needles," Dick said. His pale eyes narrowed as he recalled the seemingly senseless mumble of Janet Weems at the hospital. "Needles with roots. I can't imagine as yet what the roots might be. But I think we may find out at the radio tower."

CHAPTER VIII

Leaning Tower

The Portland radio station was like most in the country. There were the glass-walled broadcasting chambers and the larger rooms where the audience could watch through sound-proofed windows and hear through an amplifier.

It was two o'clock in the morning when Justice, Inc., got there, but the place was fairly full.

It was the vogue at the moment to conclude night parties with a visit to the station and an earful of dance music.

Smitty and Mac were a little behind the others as they entered the building housing the station.

"Needles with rrroots," burred Mac. When he was deeply puzzled or moved, he had a tendency to roll his r's. "I can't see what needles with roots have to do with a broadcastin' station."

Smitty had been increasingly thoughtful since leaving the airport.

"A radio tower looks a little like a needle," the giant

said slowly. "A great big needle sticking up into the sky—"

"Sure," said Mac sardonically, "with a root on it!"

"Well, there's a ground cable, isn't there?" snapped Smitty.

"Is there?" said Mac, who left all things electrical to the huge fellow with the china-blue eyes.

"A ground cable," worried Smitty. "And a radio tower, like a great big needle—"

Something huge and breathless, some blinding flash of intuition as to what this was all about, was almost edging into the door of his brain. But he couldn't quite get it.

They all went into the audience chamber of the broadcasting station and sat down. Through the heavy glass between them and Studio B they could see an announcer at a microphone.

The man was standing there with a script in his hand, and with the little preliminary smile on his lips affected by those who try hard to project their personality over the ether waves.

"Good morning, folks," the announcer said. "It is now exactly two o'clock, and you are about to hear some of your favorite music as arranged by Jimmy Truetone and played by Jimmy's orchestra. We'll hope this broadcast will not be interrupted as was the one at midnight."

The man's lips retained the shape of their smile, but for a moment lost its spirit. However, his voice continued to be smooth and carefree, with an implicit chuckle in it.

"Everything's normal, now, after the little power tie-up. You know, folks, that was a funny thing. It looks as if it is to become the studio mystery—a mystery that our radio experts are unable to explain. Anyway, they haven't explained it yet. All the power tubes blew at once, and the program went dead. And that's their only comment on the matter. I could tell as much about it myself, and your announcer is no radio expert, folks."

He glanced at the control man, who good-naturedly shook his fist, grinned, and went on.

"There's a story around here that somebody saw a crazy gorilla or something go up the radio tower. Maybe it was the monkey that blew the works. If so, folks, there will be no more monkey business. Take it, Jimmy."

The music of the Truetone orchestra faded in, and a girl stepped with a bright smile to the mike to go into a torch number with the repetition of the chorus.

Smitty nudged Benson suddenly and pointed furtively. Sitting ahead of them, and as yet seemingly unaware of their presence in the back row, was a man alone. It was the man who had run into the power plant at Marville, Ohio, with the tale of seeing Nevlo blasted into a mad, crippled thing.

"Pretty long hop from Marville to Portland," Smitty whispered. "And you wouldn't think a power-plant roustabout had the dough to go traveling around like that."

Benson nodded, eyes like chips of stainless steel in his dead face.

"Watch him, Smitty. When he leaves here, trail him and see where he goes. Report to me on your belt radio."

He was gone, then. And his disappearance was almost as swift and simple as the sentence. He was there, instructing Smitty, and then he wasn't there, and his exit was pointed by the soft closing of the door. The Avenger could move as silently as a ghost, and as swiftly as flickering moonlight.

Benson went to the radio tower.

It soared above him into the starry, but black, sky, a skeleton of an obelisk two hundred feet tall. But The Avenger did not look up for a moment. He looked down.

The tower had four spraddling legs, and at the foot of the leg pointing roughly northwest, about in line with the magnet's north pole, he found it. Something vaguely reminiscent of the yarn told by the man at Marville about Nevlo.

The man had said something about a blue hole in the ground, there, at the spot from which Nevlo had stumbled with a warped brain and a distorted body.

There was a blue hole here.

It was a most peculiar hole. It was perfectly concave, about two and a half feet across and five feet deep. Two deep, regular indentations encircled the hole at about the center. A certain similarity of shapes was instantly plain.

The hole looked like the shell of a standard oil drum, two and a half by five feet, with two bracing ridges around its middle. Had a drum been made of wax to reproduce a steel one faithfully, buried in hard-packed earth, then been melted carefully and pumped out, th result would have been a hole like this, cast in the ground.

The earth at the sides of the hole was fused and bluish, as if it had been exposed to tremendous heat. And if there had ever been anything in it, at least there was nothing now. Whatever had blistered the solid earth had burned any contents to nothingness; or else, if there had been traces of something, it had been removed before The Avenger arrived on the scene.

Benson looked up, then, having examined the ground first.

Far overhead, like a red star, burned the warning beacon placed there to keep planes from colliding with the steel skeleton. Between the red star and the man with the colorless, deadly eyes was an iron ladder, up the spindly steelwork, so thin that it seemed to have been fashioned of black cobwebs.

The Avenger began to climb the ladder.

Up he went, smoothly, effortlessly, seeming to flow along the rungs rather than laboriously climb them. A little faster than an ordinary man would have mounted a similar number of steps, he was at the top. Such was his physical condition that his breathing wasn't even accelerated.

He looked first at the beacon light.

It was a new one, standard, lens and all. And from it went new cable. Where the old light had been, the tip of the tower was pitted and burned. It looked as if some sort of super-rat had chewed the solid metal as ordinary rats chew bites out of cheese.

And the serrated edges had the same blue tinge, a fused, glazed tinge, like the hole in the earth at the foot of the structure.

It was then that the tower began to lean!

The average person would have thought at first that he was suffering from some illusion induced by the height. But The Avenger, with his perfect sense of equilibrium, knew instantly that it was no illusion, but an actual tilting of the tower.

He stared down. Even his telescopic gaze could reveal no figure at the base of the tower, so far down in the black night with nothing but the blackness of earth as a background. But he did see something.

A single blue-white flash. Someone down there was working on the slender legs with an acetylene torch, held under a shield to guard its flashing fire from other eyes.

If the tower was leaning, it must mean that at least one other leg had been seared through . . .

There was a heavy tremor, and the tower tipped some more! This time it kept on tilting. The killer on the ground had done enough!

Two hundred feet high. And on the top of that tower, like an insect on the top of a falling yardstick, was Dick Benson.

The thing was like a stage act with chairs piled ten high and an acrobat on top. Slowly, at first, the tall tower leaned, then more and more swiftly till it was rushing toward the distant ground with moaning speed.

At the very tip, Benson paused, ice-pale eyes calmly regarding the uprushing earth. Then he poised and leaped far out from the collapsing steel, into thin air!

Smitty didn't wait for the man from the Marville plant in the audience chamber. He went out a minute or so after Benson had left and took up a stand in a dark doorway.

Meanwhile, Smitty had passed the word to Mac.

The man knew by sight The Avenger, Mac, and Smitty. Benson and Smitty had left the audience room. When the fellow finally got up and made for the door, Mac did his share of keeping the man in ignorance of their visit by bending down as if he had dropped something, thus concealing his face.

The man wandered out the street door. There, he looked at a watch on his wrist and began to hurry a little. Behind him, a huge shadow detached itself from the gloom of a doorway and began to follow.

The man didn't go to a car, nor did he call a cab. He went on foot into the fringe of the city—a very dirty, poverty-stricken fringe where the lighting wasn't very good and where few pedestrians showed on the sidewalks.

It was the kind of spot where the cops tend to walk in pairs instead of patrolling alone.

The man went to a dark and dingy house at the blind end of a particularly malodorous street. Not a light showed at any window of the place, but when the man knocked lightly at a scarred door, the door was promptly opened.

He disappeared within, and Smitty drew closer.

That there *was* light within the place seemed evident; it was improbable that the occupant who had opened the door for the Marville visitor would be sitting around in pitch darkness.

Nevertheless, Smitty had made the circuit of every downstairs window without seeing a streak of light, so cleverly was inside illumination concealed, and without getting any other sign that the place was not deserted, before he got a hint of habitation.

A faint sound came to him from a basement window in the rear.

There was a rear yard, piled high with refuse. The giant crouched behind a rotten packing case next to the basement opening. Again the slight sound came to him. It was the sound of a voice, too indistinct for words to be made out.

The window was old and out of repair, like all the rest of the place. It was broken, and a rag had been stuffed into a small chink. Smitty very cautiously pulled the rag out, and found himself looking at a dark blanket. He slit an inch-long opening in that.

The basement was as dirty and unkempt as the yard. Among the tin cans and broken old furniture five or six men were standing. They were all looking at one spot.

Widening the slit in the blanket a little with his knife blade, so that he could see, too, Smitty looked in the same direction.

On a rough pallet of dirty blankets and burlap lay a girl. And at sight of her face, Smitty shut his teeth hard to restrain a betraying exclamation.

He had seen the girl before, recently, at General Hospital in New York.

For the girl was Janet Weems!

Smitty swore silently but fervidly. Janet was still in a daze. That was plain from her eyes; they still had the blank look they'd held at the hospital.

She must have been boldly snatched from the hospital and flown up here to Portland. Why she had been brought here instead of being killed, Smitty could not guess. And he didn't care. There was only one thing to think about. That was how to get her out of the place.

There were half a dozen men in the basement and no telling how many in the upstairs rooms of the place. But

Smitty hunched his huge shoulders and prepared to go into action in spite of the odds. He paused only long enough to whisper into his belt radio the report to The Avenger.

CHAPTER IX

Wings In The Night

The Avenger had shot from the top of the falling radio tower like a bird. A bird without wings.

He proceeded to remedy that at once.

He had perfected the world's most compact parachute some months before. Its bulk was unbelievably tiny. It was made of transparent stuff no thicker than the cellophane on a cigarette package. It greatly resembled cellophane, as a matter of fact, but its tensile strength was such that even Smitty couldn't take a sheet of it and rip it in his vast hands.

Folded, the parachute could rest in a flat pack under a man's coat and not be noticeable unless you knew about its being there.

The Avenger owed his life to methodical precautions, as well as to marvelous skill with hands and brain. One instance of his precaution was never to go up in a plane, no matter how short the hop or for what purpose, without wearing one of these little 'chutes.

He had put one on before ascending to locate the strange power line, then had hurried to the radio station without bothering to take it off. So he had it on now when the tower fell.

He didn't, couldn't, take the second necessary to remove his coat. So, as he plunged out into nothingness while the tower plunged beneath him, he simply spread his shoulders.

Not a big man. Not a bulky one. But the steel cables Dick had for muscles simply would not be confined when they were tensed and when his chest was expanded.

The coat ripped from tail to neck, and he pulled the ripcord. Had the tower been twenty feet lower he couldn't have made it. As it was, there was just enough height to let the 'chute save him.

He glanced swiftly around. There was no sign of the man who had brought the tower down. There wouldn't be, of course. With the first waver of the thing, he'd have raced off untraceably into the darkness.

With his eyes as calm as they were cold, and with almost no expression on his handsome face, Benson went to the nearest phone. If there was a single thought left in his brain about his narrow escape, it didn't show in any of his actions.

He phoned various radio stations in California. He asked just one question. In the recent power failure, did the power tubes of that particular station blow out?

At Los Angeles he got the answer he'd been waiting for.

"Who are you?" snapped a voice when The Avenger had put that question. "Some reporter or something? We don't want a lot of publicity on a power failure—"

"I'm not a reporter," Dick said quietly. "This is Richard Benson talking. I can give you references from—"

"Mr. Benson!" The man's voice was very, very different. "Say, *you* don't have to give references. Yes, our tubes blew with the power failure. Funny. too. Why would a failure blow the tubes? Why didn't a fuse blow first—or a transformer or something? I don't get it at all."

Benson didn't bother to explain or tell why he had asked the question.

"Send a man at once to your radio tower," he said. "Have him see if there is a peculiar, bluish hole at the base."

Back came the answer:

"Yes, Mr. Benson, there *is* such a hole at the base. The hole's in a northeast line from it. A curious round hole as if an oil drum had been buried there and then removed so carefully that it left its exact print in the hole. But how did you know—"

"Is your beacon light all right at the tip of the tower?"

"No, sir. That is completely gone, and its standard along with it. Looks as if it had been *burned* off."

The Avenger hung up.

In Portland, Maine, a tall tower had been charred by a current mightier than radio ever uses. In Los Angeles, a similar tower had been similarly treated.

He called the Montreal meteorological station.

They reported a phenomenal increase in the intensity and brilliance of the aurora borealis during the time of the power failure. It flared up with it, then died down again when it had ended. So, no doubt, a vast electrical disturbance in the Heaviside layer of earth's atmosphere, or beyond, had caused the trouble.

Benson didn't bother to point out that perhaps it had been the other way around, that perhaps the trouble had caused the electrical storm.

There was a slight vibration at his waist, from the belt radio. One of his band wanted to talk to him.

From his vest pocket came an earphone hardly larger than a quarter. Smitty's tense, low tone came to him as he put it to his ear.

"I trailed the man, chief. Nailed him at a green

house with a double porch at the foot of Vermont Avenue. He's in here now, with six or a dozen thugs around him. I'm at a basement window of the place, looking in. There's more than the man here. They've got Janet Weems! I don't know how they took her out of General, but she's here now, tied and gagged. Still out of her mind, I think. Now there's another person coming into the basement— For the love of Heaven!"

The radio went dead, as if the giant's explosive, horrified exclamation had blasted the tiny transmitter.

In the refuse-littered yard, Smitty crouched in the shadow of the packing case and glared through the slit in the blanket into the basement. His tiny radio had been forgotten in the sight that met his eyes.

"Another person coming into the basement," he had said. Now this other person was in full view.

Smitty saw a big-shouldered, bulky figure, dressed in cheap but fairly good clothing. The man swayed from side to side as he walked, with arms hanging low. He had the arm length and the walk of a gorilla.

The man turned so that the giant could see his face.

It was the face of a brute rather than a man. The eyebrows, ridged and heavy, made little pits of the black, dull eyes. The nose was flattened and smeared half to one side. The ears were masses of gristle with no resemblance whatsoever to human ears.

The man even wore his clothes as if unaccustomed to such things, as a trained bear or a great ape might wear clothes. A gorilla of a creature! He made even the hoodlums in the cellar uneasy, Smitty could see. Two of them promptly stepped back, with their arms raised a bit, when he lunged a step toward them.

But the brutish figure's destination was not the men. He started toward the girl, heavy arms crooked out in a gesture so much like a wrestler's that it would have been comical if it had not been so grim.

"*Is* it a gorilla?" Smitty whispered to himself. But he knew the answer.

It was a man, all right, inhuman as it appeared. It waddled with its wrestler's posture toward the girl who lay bound and gagged . . .

There was a ghost of sound behind Smitty. The giant turned swiftly and looked up.

A man stood behind him with a crowbar in upraised hands, just ready to flail down on Smitty's skull.

Smitty, enormous as he was, looked like the type of person who would be so muscle-bound that he'd get in his own way if he tried to sit down. But he was not that way at all.

For all his near seven feet of height and his almost three hundred pounds of brawn, he was nearly as lithe as Dick Benson himself. And he could move nearly as fast.

Now, in the split second before that murderous bar could flail down, his huge right hand shot up, and his big body eeled to one side.

The bar came down with dissipated force on his shoulder, instead of full strength on his hand. Under his colossal pads of muscles, he felt dull pain. And he didn't like it.

Meanwhile, his right hand had found its mark, which was the man's throat.

The man didn't raise the bar again, nor did he make any noise, though doubtless he would have made a lot of strange and anguished noises if Smitty's hand hadn't been pressing his neck into a thing that could have been fitted by a size 10 collar.

The bar dropped, and the man would have followed, save that Smitty had risen from his crouch and held him upright.

A minute would have been enough. But Smitty, still angered by the stinging in his shoulder, held him for two. And when the man dropped, he fell in such a way that you knew he would never again rise under his own power. The Avenger never took a human life. But his aides did, now and then, when the provocation was sufficiently great.

Smitty loped to the back door. It was open a crack. He bent over, so that his great height shouldn't betray him, and became simply an anonymous shadow in the night.

"Okay out there?" came a whisper from somebody peering out the slightly opened door. "Anybody say something? Or was it a cat?"

So his exclamation at the sight of the warped figure entering the basement had given him away, Smitty gathered. It had been heard and a man sent to investigate. Well, he would be investigating the sulphur situation in hell at about this moment.

"Okay out there, now," he whispered back, truthfully enough.

He opened the door, not too swiftly or urgently.

It opened onto a pitch-black hall or corridor, instead of a room. Barely to be seen was the dim white blotch of a man's face in the darkness.

But Smitty, silhouetted against the stars, was more easily to be observed.

There was a gasp as the man inside noticed the unfamiliar size of the one who opened the door. The gasp was preliminary to a shout. But the shout was never uttered.

Smitty's right hand took up its throttling task on a new throat. It shot forward for the neck under that dim white blotch of a face and found it comfortably.

This time Smitty had no personal animosity exaggerating the power in his huge fingers. He calculated time by counting slowly to himself, as calmly as if he were timing a soft-boiled egg, and he opened his hand with the count of fifty. Slow. This fellow would probably breathe again. Smitty wouldn't have gone so far as to guarantee that, but *probably* he would.

The giant went down the dark hall, as softly as if he were a little Nellie Gray instead of the towering giant he was. One small slot of light showed in the otherwise all-prevailing darkness.

This was a crack that came from another door, halfway down the corridor. He went to it and saw that it was the basement door.

Ahead of him, in a room at the front of the house, he heard a low rumble of guarded voices. Several men in there. No telling how many.

He opened the basement door and started down the stairs. Then he paused, lips stony.

The stairs were of the half-finished type with no risers between the treads. And there was no partition between stairs and basement.

It was a little like an ordinary ladder, slanted more than most, descending into the cellar. There wasn't a chance of getting down that unseen.

Smitty peered down and to the side.

There, from this other angle, was the scene he had witnessed through the slit cut in the light-concealing blanket at the basement window.

Seven men—counting the shambling, appalling figure that looked like a mad gorilla—and a girl. The strange figure was beside the girl now; and the misshapen, fumbling hands were touching her smooth arms.

"Attaboy, Nevlo," laughed one of the others, "show the gal you may not look like much, but you sure are a big-time Romeo!"

A kind of glare came into Smitty's eyes. Like most big men, he had a large regard for the rights of those smaller and weaker than he. It made him see red when someone was shoved around.

And there couldn't have been a more outstanding example of it than this: a girl, bound, helpless, dazed of brain, with six men around to slap her down if she tried to do anything—and a seventh, like a damned gorilla, now roughing her up!

Smitty's hand went to his left-hand coat pocket. In the pocket was one of MacMurdie's brilliant chemical inventions. It was a small glass pellet containing a gas that paralyzed movement.

It was the weirdest thing. The victim kept his clarity of mind and could see and hear all right, but he couldn't move. The motor muscles were left without control.

Smitty poised the pellet to toss it down to break on the cellar floor. And somebody kicked his elbow.

The glass pill dropped and broke on the floor next to Smitty, as he had scrambled to his feet and stared up.

A man had got up to him, sneaking down the hall from the front room where Smitty had heard voices. The man loomed over him now, snarling, murderous.

"Throw a stink-bomb or somethin', will ya?" the man howled. "Well, see how you like hot lead!"

His hand started for his gun, but didn't get to where it was holstered. His arm and hand seemed to wither and droop, like a plant stem in a drought. And then the man himself sagged slowly to the floor.

He stared at Smitty with horrified perplexity in his eyes. Smitty knew just how he felt. He could see the giant, but he couldn't do anything about it. He suddenly had mush for muscles. He couldn't even get out of the way if Smitty tried to crown him. The gas was working!

But Smitty wasted no time on the man. He was holding his breath and facing the stairs. They'd heard the other's howl, down there, and were rushing up to look into the matter!

Smitty's fist got the first one and he fell back, spilling three others as he did so. But a fourth, holding himself far to one side, escaped the tumble and lunged upward. He got the giant by the ankles, and Smitty fell.

The house shook. So did the stairs. For Smitty had

fallen so that he joined the rest at the foot of the steps in a scrambling, unlovely tangle.

What he didn't know was that fragments of the glass pellet rode down with him on his coat tail, and that with the fragments were evaporating droplets of the terrifically concentrated liquid which made the numbing gas.

So Smitty drew in a deep breath as he got two men with a hand on the neck of each.

Drew in the breath and felt instantly as if he had been drained of all strength.

He knew at once what had happened then. But it was too late. He held his breath again to keep from inhaling any more of the stuff, but the one whiff had almost paralyzed him. He could just barely keep his hands on the two throats and raise a weak foot to keep back a third man who was trying to crawl over prone bodies and get at him.

The only saving feature of the thing was that the precious gang of killers in here were as bad off as he was.

No! They weren't. Not all of them. Smitty suddenly saw, with a sense of doom in his heart that could not be translated into action, that a man down there at the other end of the basement was not under the numbing spell of the gas.

This one stood next to the bound girl and the mad gorilla form. The gas would get down there soon, but the stuff hadn't reached him yet. He was perfectly capable of drawing his gun—and was doing so.

Smitty, dragging toward the fellow with hopeless slowness like a leaden-footed person in a nightmare, saw a .38 automatic come forth in a leisurely, unhurried way. In the same manner, it leveled at his head.

Not at his body, which was protected by a bulletproof garment of The Avenger's devising—but at his head!

Smitty saw a cold, dark eye behind the gunsight, saw a cold, tooth-revealing grin on the lips under the eye, saw the muzzle of the .38 yawn like a thing capable of being mounted on a battleship's turret.

He saw sure death!

And then he saw the man abruptly collapse, with a small gash suddenly appearing on the exact top of his skull. It was as if someone had suddenly clubbed him down. Only there was no one around to club him.

CHAPTER X

Murder Mansion

The Avenger, as has been said, never took human life. In his extreme youth, when he was piling up a fortune in far corners of the earth, he had been forced to kill a man. The memory of that still bit and cut.

Instead of killing, therefore, he disabled—as that man who had been about to murder Smitty was disabled.

Benson had two weapons that at first glance didn't seem to amount to much when stacked up against the machine guns and pineapple bombs of the underworld.

One was a razor-edged, needle-pointed little knife with a hollow tube for a handle—one of the world's best throwing knives. This, Dick holstered at the calf of his left leg and called, with chilling affection, Ike.

Mike was holstered below his right knee. Mike was a slim little .22, specially built, with only a slight curve for a handle and with a cylinder holding only four cartridges to keep it streamlined and small. Mike had a silencer, so that when he spoke he whispered politely.

But with each whisper a man went down.

The man went down—not dead, but creased, hit glancingly on the top of the head so that he was stunned instead of killed. It was a shot requiring eighth-inch precision, but one that Benson had mastered to perfection.

At the basement window, where he had stopped on his encirclement of the house to which Smitty's call had drawn him, he had pressed Mike's diminutive trigger just in time.

Smitty and all the rest seemed helpless to move very far in the basement, so Benson left the window at once and ran to the rear door and into the house.

Smitty tried to yell to him and found that his voice came out only in a weak cry like that of a hungry baby. His vocal cords were still numbed, as was all the rest of him.

What he was trying to yell to Benson was to hurry back to that window because the one man in the cellar not so much affected by the numbing gas because of distance was getting away.

And that one was the shambling figure that wore man's clothes almost as an animal would wear them.

Smitty, in helpless agony, watched the misshapen figure hoist itself to the window and squeeze through. It was a tight fit, but it made it.

Smitty feebly cursed the freak of ill fortune that had exposed him to the gas. He was trying to drag himself to the window and after the fugitive when Benson came down the stairs.

Dick had had a little trouble with the men upstairs. Four of them lay on the hall floor, to testify to their end of that trouble; The Avenger had been delayed about four minutes to testify to his end.

"Chief!" gasped Smitty, in the suffocated voice and slurred tone that was all his paralyzed throat muscles would permit. "Guy like gorilla . . . Nevlo . . . got away."

"Nevlo?" snapped Benson, eyes like ice with little lights behind them, but otherwise not seeming much concerned.

"Yes . . . got away . . . basement window. Guy who's crazy . . . can ruin the world. We're sunk!"

"No," said The Avenger, voice cold and without emotion, "we're not sunk. Nellie came with me. She's outside, posted in advance to take care of just such an emergency. She can take up the trail and radio us when it ends."

In the night outside, Nellie took up the chase. Only one man had come out of the house after The Avenger had gone in, so she'd had no choice to make as to which of several to follow.

Like a lovely little shadow, she slid along after the lumbering, inhuman-looking figure that had emerged from the basement window.

As she went, she felt horror mount in her heart. This was surely the man named Nevlo, according to the descriptions of the thing he had become since that blinding flash near the Marville power plant. Nevlo! With a secret more destructive than any man had ever possessed before! And he was most certainly demented!

You could tell that by his shambling walk. You could hear it in the mumbling, incoherent words he kept muttering aloud to himself.

Nevlo!

A madman, but sane enough, it seemed, to work with others. The trail ended at a quite expensive-looking coupé in which another man sat at the driver's seat and waited.

Nevlo climbed in when the door was opened for him. Nellie heard an inquiring voice, then Nevlo's mumble, and then a curse. Though she had been unable to hear words, she could divine the meaning of the short passage.

The man at the wheel, whoever he was, had asked

what had gone on at the house back there and had been told that things went wrong.

The car drove off, gaining speed rapidly in the night and heading south. And Nellie had cause to be thankful that it was big and expensive and rode easily because she was accompanying the two, hiding in the luggage compartment under the rear deck of the coupé.

Nellie had thought that she was playing in luck when she felt the compartment handle and found it unlocked, so that she was able to crawl in while the gorilla person entered the car. But long before she left the compartment again, she concluded that she was completely out of luck.

First off, she was locked in! Then she was kept in for a couple of years. At least, it seemed like years.

She had crawled into the thing just as dawn was lighting the east. Through a crack in the bottom near the side, she saw the whirling road beneath her more and more clearly as dawn progressed. It was about half-past five in the morning, she concluded, when the car stopped for gas.

She heard the gas-tank cap unscrewed and the bump of the nozzle as the attendant shoved it into the gooseneck. Then she heard something else that made her heart skip a beat.

A hand on the handle of the compartment door!

The handle turned, and the door lifted, and she prepared to follow the old melodrama days and sell her life dearly.

But the door was only lifted an inch, then banged down. The lock shut as a key was turned in it. So then she had plenty to think about.

Had the car's driver noticed that someone was lurking inside, when he opened the deck door that inch? Had he slammed the thing shut and locked it to keep that somebody a prisoner till a nice murder spot presented itself?

Or had the driver just idly tried the catch, discovered it unlocked, and fastened it again to guard his spare tire from theft?

Nellie would know which of the two theories was correct, of course, with the passage of time. But the uncertainty didn't tend to make that passage any faster or easier.

And even if she had been easy in her mind and prepared with a radio and a couple of good books, the time would still have seemed long. Because it was long.

She whirled along in that luggage compartment till she lost all track of hours, but she judged it must be at least noon. Then the coupé stopped.

It stayed stopped, while Nellie tried to relax in the cramped quarters and couldn't. Then it started again.

Through the crack in the bottom she saw the road gradually darken. She was past seeing or feeling, almost, when the coupé stopped again.

"For dinner, I suppose," she thought resentfully. "And I haven't even had any breakfast!"

The whole trip had seemed aimless and slow, as if the driver were trying to kill time and not get to his destination till dark. If so, he was successful, for it was full night when the car rolled over gravel somewhere and finally came to a definite halt.

Nellie felt the car sag twice as the two inside got out. She heard wind in trees and men's voices and the crunch of their steps in the gravel. Then she was left alone.

She could have gotten out of the compartment at any time, but not without noise. The only way she could do it was to take a screwdriver from the tool kit in the compartment, put it under the lockbar—exposed on the inside—and pry. She hadn't dared try that all during the day, even while the car was in motion. But she had to attempt it, now, noise or no noise. She couldn't stay in here forever.

She got out the screwdriver, pried, and the belt flew

back with a sound like that of a small gun. She pushed the lid up.

Her luck was apparently good. She did not look out into a yawning gun muzzle or even a yawning face. There was no one around. She put the lid down in place again and slid for a big tree, twenty feet to her right, to hide awhile and look things over.

Some of the sound she had thought was wind in the trees was the sound of water. Waves on a rough coast. There was a tang of salt in the air. So she knew she was next to the shore.

All around her were trees. It was like a forest, save that a forest hasn't velvety, expensively trimmed lawn through it. Not a forest, then. An estate along the ocean.

Far down a dimly seen graveled drive, through many interlacing branches, she caught glimpses of headlights as a car rolled along the winding highway. At about the same time, out from where she heard the waves on rocks, she caught a lighthouse gleam. Its timing placed her, versed as she was, in all the things an air pilot should know.

She was at Bar Harbor, on some great estate. And the knowledge didn't please her.

Bar Harbor is so exclusive that sometimes it even resents itself. Its estates are set so far back from the main roads, with so many trees intervening between highway and houses, that you could live, raise a family, and die without anyone outside the grounds ever being any wiser.

Nellie didn't care for such privacy, just now. It meant that no matter what might happen to her, a call for help would be as much ignored as if she were on the Sahara miles from the nearest sheik.

To her right was the big house belonging to the forestlike grounds. It was of gray stone with a red tile roof. It probably contained a modest thirty rooms and an army of servants. It was, Nellie thought, a very strange place indeed for the crippled, mind-blasted Nevlo to have come. And to have come, furthermore, straight from a gang lair.

Drawing a deep breath, Nellie left the kindly shelter of the tree and slipped toward the great bulk of the house.

There was a dog. He was a big dog and looked as if he hated the world. He came around a corner of the house and glared at Nellie with his hackles rising and his muzzle snarling back preparatory to a lot of barking and a mad attack.

Nellie sat down.

Vague curiosity mingled with ferocity in the dog's glare. He had never seen anybody do that before, when he threatened to rush. He came closer, stiff-legged, and Nellie sighed with relief. She knew her dogs.

In a minute her fingers were cautiously scratching around his ears, and the angry hackles were going down. She got up and began going around the house, with the dog trotting uncertainly after her.

She looked in every window on the ground floor. No sign of Nevlo or the coupé's driver there. The kitchen door beckoned her. It was early, and there was a chance that the door was unlocked.

She went to it. Fido was getting suspicious again, but his suspicions were laid a second time when Nellie walked boldly, but noiselessly, to the door, opened it, and went in as if she belonged there.

She got through the kitchen and up the back stairs to the second floor. There, she went from room to room, like a lovely little shadow. And still she didn't see Nevlo or the other man. She saw several servants, heard several more behind closed doors, and saw the master of the house in the second-floor library. But that was all.

The owner of the house had been placed for her by a letter she had seen lying on a table. Jerome Hooley. It was a name to conjure with. Hooley was a utilities magnate

87

with a twenty-two-room penthouse in New York for winters and this big place at Bar Harbor for summers. He was a very wealthy, very influential, man.

Observed unaware by the unseen visitor in his house, Hooley didn't look impressive. He was small, elderly, with a wizened, fretful look, swathed in a quilted dressing gown as if the cool breeze from the ocean were more than his thin blood could stand.

But Nellie wasn't there to observe Hooley. She was there to find where Nevlo had gone and what he was up to. And she drew blank on both. She'd thought the two from the coupé had come into the house. Apparently they'd hidden in an outbuilding.

Nellie went downstairs again. At the foot, she stopped suddenly and listened. It seemed to her she had heard a furtive footstep, behind her.

A *dragging* footstep, as if whatever had made it had been crippled.

There was no more sound, though, so she concluded she had imagined it. She went on to the kitchen.

The refrigerator enticed her. Since dinner last night, she had eaten nothing. She opened it and took out a nice chicken leg and a steak tail. The leg was for her, the steak tail for Fido, to keep him silent.

She stepped into the night, munching on the chicken leg. And out of the darkness came arms!

They seemed two yards long and made of steel. One went around her waist like a coil of ship's cable. The other clamped around her throat, and a big hand slapped over her mouth and nostrils.

Nellie could handle big men with her dexterity in jujitsu. But she had to have *some* sort of warning. This time she had none whatever. Furthermore, she could sense from the way the arms held her that they were versed in jujitsu, too—enough to guard against it a little.

She tried to bite the hand over her lips and was

unable to. She tried to squirm loose and couldn't manage that, either. Meanwhile, she was being carried.

The thing holding her bore her through thickets and between trees, and the salty tang in the air grew stronger.

Nellie was being held so that she could look ahead and see where they were going. She wished she couldn't, for their destination was the edge of the cliff shooting up from the sea.

They got to the edge. Darkness of night was over her, ahead of her, and, for about a hundred feet, *underneath* her. Down there, she could see frothing white lines now and then as slow surf broke on jagged rock.

She didn't have much time to muse on rock or surf. The thing holding her swung her far out and released her. She began falling—falling toward rock and sea!

CHAPTER XI

Picture Of Terror!

At Bleek Street, after a plane hop from Portland, The Avenger took a two-inch case from his pocket. It was about the size and shape of a girl's compact. But it was not a compact. It was a camera, with a lens to make any optician mumble with joy.

"Pictures, huh?" said Smitty. "What of?"

"The basement back at the Portland house," said Dick Benson, taking out the tiny roll of film.

"Pictures of the basement?"

"Yes. One reason why I delayed using Mike on the man aiming at you was that I was taking pictures through the slit you cut in the blanket."

Smitty wanted to ask what the pictures were of. But he throttled his curiosity. Benson went into the developing room and came back. And then Smitty saw the subject.

The pictures were of the gorilla-like individual whose fumbling attentions to the bound girl in the basement had driven Smitty into charging the mob.

There was one of the men bending near the girl, with clumsy, misshapen hands on her bound arms. There was one of him staring straight toward the camera with lips drawn back from snarling teeth. There was one of him loping toward the window and the camera, with long arms down so that the hands almost scraped the cellar floor. Finally, there was one of him crouching a little, arms out crookedly, as if to gather in an opponent and crack his spine in a bear hug.

"Nice guy," said Smitty, scowling. "He'd be nicer in a zoo, though. You sure got some good shots of him."

"I needed some good shots," said Benson quietly. "You saw the fellow more clearly than I did, perhaps. How would you describe his coloring?"

"Black eyes," said Smitty. "Dull, reddish complexion, not very healthy-looking. Black hair with a couple of thin gray streaks in it."

The Avenger nodded. "That is about the way I had it marked down."

He went into a corner where a great cabinet stood. From the cabinet he got a small case that looked a bit like an overnight bag. And the presence of the case explained to Smitty why Benson had taken such pains to get pictures of the gorilla-man.

In that case was probably the world's most complete and subtle make-up collection.

In the top lid there was a small but perfect mirror. In the top tray there were dozens of pairs of tissue-thin glass cups designed to fit over The Avenger's eyeballs. Each pair was just a little different in tint from all the others. Under the top tray were wigs, pigments for achieving all known tints of complexion, substances for changing the flare of the nostrils or the set of the jaw— everything known in the way of disguises, plus a few that The Avenger had thought up himself and which were unknown to others.

Dick Benson was a make-up artist, unsurpassed, and

Smitty watched his calm but swift proceedings with the awe he always felt on such an occasion.

Next to the mirror in the lid, The Avenger fastened with thumbtacks an enlargement of the picture showing the crouching man head-on. Twisted ruin of a countenance; dark, bitter eyes; nose smeared to one side—the wreck of a thing that seemed once to have been intelligent.

Then Benson's expert fingers began applying plastics to his own features, while he stared first into the mirror at himself and then at the picture right next to it.

Smitty shook his head a little, incredulously.

"I thought even you couldn't make up to resemble Nevlo," he said.

"The more unique the face," The Avenger pointed out, "the easier it is to follow its lines. It's only when a face has little character that it's hard to simulate it."

Over the pale and deadly eyeballs went little glass cups with black pupils painted on them. Deftly he lined faint, iron-gray streaks in his own thick black hair.

Benson stood up, almost unconsciously simulating the crouching, gorilla-like posture of the fellow in the pictures.

Josh Newton came into the big room.

"I phoned all the electric-utilities heads you told me to," he said. "Eight of them, counting Blake of Cleveland. Among them they just about own the public utilities of North America."

"What did you find out?" said Benson, putting on shoes with inch-and-a-half lifts to give him extra height, which he immediately discounted by his crouching gait.

"Four of them I couldn't get any information on," said Josh. "I was simply told that they were out of town, no address. Blake, I found, was in his Cleveland home. The other three had just left, their, secretaries said, for Cleveland."

"Each of the three of them?"

Josh nodded. "Looks almost as if there were to be a convention of power executives in Cleveland. Anyhow, that's where they all headed."

"The others, the ones you couldn't trace, will be there, too," Dick said emotionlessly. "I was pretty sure of it before. But I wanted you to check on it. Smitty, we're going west by plane. You will go to Marville, to Plant 4, and search for a dead man."

"Huh?" said the giant.

"You may not find one, of course. But search for a recently murdered man, anyhow. I'd suggest that you start with the plant itself, and then widen your field of investigation gradually from that point. It will be safer if you don't let anyone see you looking around."

Benson went out. Down on the second floor was a huge wardrobe containing hundreds of suits, good and bad, fine and ragged. Smitty and Josh knew that he was going to select the type of thing Nevlo had worn—rather cheap clothing that didn't fit too well.

Smitty and Josh stared at each other.

"What's in the wind?" said Smitty, perplexed.

Josh shrugged. "He's taking Nevlo's place somewhere. That's plain enough. But I don't know what it's all about."

"Didn't he say anything to you when he told you to go phoning around the country about utilities magnates?"

Josh rubbed his jaw.

"He said something about this power-failure business being destructive only, that it could not be used constructively in any way. That's all."

"It doesn't make sense to me," worried Smitty. "And this job of mine! I'm to go to Marville and hunt for a dead man. What dead man? And what made him dead? And when was he killed and by whom?"

"Probably," said Josh, "those are the things you are to find out. Good hunting!"

The coast of Maine, along the Bar Harbor sector, is as uneven and ragged as a fringe of ancient lace.

There are sheer cliffs rising smooth from the water to their crest. There are fields of house-sized boulders breaking the surf into fragments in other spots. There are shallow pools in which water is left when the tide retreats. There are deep potholes, formed over the centuries by whirlpool action of the tides.

At the foot of the cliff on which Hooley's home was built, the ragged-lace appearance was pronounced. Staring down, you saw white foam interspersed with irregular black spots. Some of the black spots were rounded rocks; some were pools, either shallow or deep.

That was the picture that presented itself to Nellie Gray as she hurtled down toward death like a plummet, thrown over the cliff's top by the gorilla arms that had held her.

There was a solid line of white where the last ramparts of the surf were shattered against the solid foot of the cliff itself, then the black spots. And right under her was one of the larger dark patches.

They say you can see your whole life in retrospect in a second when death faces you. That may or may not be true. But it is a fact that thought is so accelerated that a whole chain of life can be encompassed in a wink of an eye.

It was so in Nellie's case.

Most of her brain was shocked with the paralyzing fear of death which even the bravest person carries. The instinct to live is strong; the fear of death is correspondingly strong.

But in another small corner of her mind, she was thinking fast—and staring down at the larger black spot.

That might be an extra big, extra-flat-topped rock. Or it might be a pool beyond the first fringe of surf. If it happened to be a pool, it might be six inches deep . . . or it might be twenty feet deep.

In any event, Nellie was turning lithely in air like a cat and straightening out like the expert diver she was; she was heading for the black patch. Literally, she was heading for it, diving down like a comet with her arms out in a swan-dive spread.

There was a breathless half-second when she was going to hit. Then the blackness reflected a single glint of starlight, showing that it was a pool, all right.

And then she struck!

Luck helps those who are strong and competent and can help themselves. Not one woman in thousands could have turned a fall into a perfect dive and hit so small a bull's-eye. And, as if in recompense, the bull's-eye turned out to be a pool with just enough depth to do the trick.

It's rock, after all, Nellie thought wildly, as she struck. But she had forgotten the terrific impact that ordinary water presents at a height of a hundred feet. Then she was slanting briefly down and up again in the shallowest possible of dives, and her head bobbed above the ebony surface.

It took her a moment to realize that she wasn't dead, another to feel that she hadn't escaped free, after all, because her left leg was numb from dragging briefly on the bottom. Then she lay on the rim of the pool, oblivious of the cold spray that occasionally broke over her. Her lips were moving a little, prayerfully. It was the closest call she had ever had.

In a very short time, though, she eyed the cliff with her firm chin determined. She was going to go back up that cliff and confront Nevlo again—

Some faint sound from offshore caught her ear. She stared out and saw a dark bulk.

A lot of looking, and twisting around so that the

stars could silhouette bits of it at a time, showed her that the bulk was a seaplane.

It was without lights. But there was somebody aboard. Because, now that her attention was on it, she could hear low voices for a moment. Then silence.

And now there was a noise from the side toward the cliff. She stared in that direction and instantly crawled behind a boulder where the white of the surf helped to hide the light gray of her torn dress.

Somebody was coming down the cliff!

She heard rocks rattle as the descent was completed, heard a splash as somebody stepped into water. Then she saw a figure coming toward her.

It was the crouching, misshapen Nevlo!

"Hurry up!" came a voice from near where Nellie had heard the rocks rattle. Nevlo had a companion, it seemed. Probably the man who had driven the coupé.

"I can't find her," said Nevlo, almost at Nellie's elbow. She was taut, ready for the man, now, if he should see her.

"Let her alone. She's dead—smashed in a hundred pieces."

"I can't find her body—"

"It probably bounced out into the surf. She had a light dress on; you wouldn't be able to see it in the foam. Come *on*!"

The gorilla form turned, one foot almost stepping on Nellie's left hand, and went away. Nellie heard the sound of a boat. There was a short interval; then she heard the subdued take-off of the seaplane. The motor was evidently muffled. Nevlo, or the other, had boarded the plane from the boat.

From the spot where the plane had been, she heard the boat again. But it did not return to shore at this point. It went on down the coast, till its soft purring faded into the distance.

Nellie found the cliff path and climbed up. The big dog

met her almost the minute she scrambled up over the edge. He was still uncertain about her, but it would not have mattered now whether he barked or not. If he had, the sound would have been lost in the uproar coming from the house.

Screams, yells of men, and one high shriek: "The police! Get the police!"

She hurried to the gray stone structure. As she neared it, through a long French window, she could see the forms of people gathered in one room on her side. She went to the window and stared in.

He lay on the floor of that room—Hooley, utilities baron and owner of the estate. He had been murdered, but not just neatly put out of the world of the living.

The man lay in a red lake, looking as if a cageful of lions had been at him. He was literally torn to pieces. It seemed impossible that a human could have done that. It must have been an animal—or a man who crouched and moved like a gorilla and whose long arms, as Nellie knew from first-hand information, had a gorilla's strength.

CHAPTER XII

Power Ring

In any industry, if you trace origins and control closely enough, you find the channels leading more and more indirectly to fewer and fewer hands. Eventually, it becomes clear that a very small handful of men are the rulers of that industry.

It was so with electric power.

The seven men who were meeting in Blake's Cleveland home, along with Blake himself, who was no pygmy in the business, could have caused almost as complete a power blackout as the strange failures that had already come to pass, if they had cared to. For they controlled almost all the power companies in North America.

Almost all—not quite. One empire was not represented here, because the emperor happened to be dead—that one being Hooley, of Bar Harbor.

There was a man named Jerand Jarvis, and another named Robert Vance; there were James J. Guest, Marvin

Masters, Hall Singer, Pierpont Ryan and, of course, John Blake, their host.

They were the utilities masters of North America, powerful, wealthy, the final authority on electric power for a continent. But they didn't look like masters at the moment. They looked like very bewildered, frightened men.

Some of them looked scared into a blue funk. Some seemed snarlingly angry at their own fear and the thing that had caused it. But all, no matter what their outward reactions, were obviously terrified.

"When's he coming, anyway?" snapped Jerand Jarvis, a stout gentleman who looked as if he had to guard against gout and apoplexy.

Pierpont Ryan, a red-headed man with gray beginning to lighten his hair, but with advancing age not doing a thing to ameliorate his quick temper, glared at Blake.

"You're responsible for this, Blake. You hired Nevlo in the first place. And then you fired him. Why didn't you take him back when he threatened you with a power shutoff of Plant 4—and then went ahead and proved he could cause it?"

"I simply didn't believe he was able to do such a thing," said Blake. "Think a minute of the impossibility of it! Never in the history of electricity has a man been able to do the things that Nevlo claims he can do."

"Claims?" snorted Ryan. "He *can* do it. He did it, didn't he? He made your damned Plant 4 useless. And then, twice recently, he went far beyond that and cut off *all* power. Claim be damned!"

"Why didn't you get in touch with Nevlo and do something before things reached such a state?" added James Guest, a lanky Westerner, whose empire took in eight states.

"I couldn't find him," protested Blake. "I tried to do just that, but Nevlo wouldn't get in touch with me. Then, when he did, just recently—"

"Then it was too late," Ryan finished for him. "Then he got in touch with you only to demand that you call us together here and allow him to make some preposterous blackmail claim against us. Well, I'm warning you now that *I* won't pay any blackmail."

"Gentlemen, gentlemen!" urged Marvin Masters. "Please! This isn't getting us anywhere. Blake may or may not be responsible for the situation in which we find ourselves. Nevlo may or may not be preposterous in his claim against us. The thing for us to discuss is causes, not results."

Blake nodded.

"Also," he said heavily, "we'd better resign ourselves to the fact that he's got us just where he wants us. I don't have to tell you how many millions of dollars just one day's shutdown of all our plants would cost us, or describe the catastrophes that would result from such a shutdown in hospitals and factories and subways. It is pretty evident that the most colossal sum he can try to extort must be carefully considered by us."

Ryan's choleric face expressed an insanity of fury. It was evident that he was driven almost out of his mind by the fact that some outside power had, momentarily, complete control over him. Obviously, he wasn't used to being controlled by anything but his own dictates.

However, it was no good being enraged. Blake's logic was sound, if comfortless.

"What do you suppose he'll ask?"

Blake moistened his lips in the anguish that comes to any money man commanded to part with a large sum.

"He intimated to me, when he ordered me to get in touch with you gentlemen, that he would ask forty or fifty million dollars."

"Fif—" gasped Guest. "The man's mad!"

Blake nodded unhappily. "Mad, of course. Which makes our situation all the more hopeless. No sane man would shut off all power and allow the human suffering bound to result, for money. It takes a madman to do such a thing. If Nevlo were sane, we might be able to reason with him. Mad, he is beyond reason. There is left for us only to do as he says—or take the consequences."

The door opened, and Blake's butler poked his head in. The man's face was pale, and his eyes bulged with fear.

"He is here, Mr. Blake. Nevlo."

Instantly the room became so still that the sound of Ryan's choleric breathing seemed loud. Then Blake's ragged sigh sounded out.

"Show him in, Pearson."

They all heard it. The dragging, shuffling steps of a person crippled and abnormal. The ill-timed steps that indicated a mental disorder as well as a physical imbalance.

The steps paused outside the door, and then the maker of the steps came into the room.

Bitter black eyes, a face that looked like the heavy-boned countenance of a gorilla, arms that hung so low they almost touched the floor, lips moving constantly in a soundless muttering.

"Here are the men you wanted to see, Nevlo," said Blake. His face was strained in an effort not to show the fear and hate and disgust expressed more openly on the faces of the others. His tone was deliberately calm, almost soothing. "Tell us, now, just what you want."

Harsh words came from the crouching, monstrous form by the door, while the vindictive black eyes went from one man to another of that tense group.

"What do I want?" came the harsh words. "Plenty, gentlemen. I grew up in the power business. I helped it reach the position it has today. My inventions are in use all over the land. I was the one who laid out Plant 4. And what was my reward? I was discharged like any dollar-an-hour electrician! I was cast aside on the junk heap. But I knew too much to stay on the junk heap." Wild laughter came from the mumbling, stiff-looking lips. "I have proved that. And now I will have my revenge—and a fortune."

"Yes, yes, you'll have your revenge," said Blake soothingly. "But precisely what is your demand, Nevlo?"

They all stared with bated breath at the monstrous, crippled figure.

"My demand?" said Nevlo. "This is it. I want five million dollars, cash, before tomorrow night. If I don't get it, all power goes off tomorrow at midnight."

Blake's gasp could be heard loudly in the room as he stared at the gorilla-like figure. The other men suddenly buzzed excited whispers at each other. There was an air of tremendous relief in the room.

Five million. It was a huge sum. But it was so much less than the men had feared would be demanded that it plainly seemed almost reasonable to them.

Ryan, by concerted whispers and nods, became spokesman. He had reconsidered his resolve to pay no blackmail.

"We'll meet that demand, Nevlo. You will get your five million dollars before tomorrow night. But in return we shall expect you to show us how you are able to shut off power in such a wholesale manner. We must know, so that we can guard against it in the future. We can't face such demands as this every few months—"

The butler stuck his head in the door again. Blake glared at him. But the glare was wasted. The butler wasn't even looking at his master. He eyed all of them, helplessly, fearfully, and bleated:

"I . . . sirs . . . good heavens! There is *another* Nevlo here!"

A chair crashed as Blake sprang up, mouth open with amazement and terror.

"Pearson, you're mad! Another Nevlo—"

The butler was shoved violently aside, and into the room waddled a second monstrous gorilla figure.

Line for line, its face was the same as the first Nevlo's face. In posture, movement, and in every other way, here were twin monstrosities.

Ryan's profane exclamation ripped out:

"Here's a fine one! Which is which? What the hell *is* this, anyhow?"

A scream of rage and fright came from the writhing lips of the second visitor. He turned and fled away down the hall.

And after him went the first one.

As The Avenger pursued the misshapen being who had come to Blake's home just a few minutes too soon, he took from his eyeballs the tinted eye cups that made black eyes of his colorless orbs. He couldn't see very well through them, and there was, in addition, the risk of their being broken in any violent struggle and impairing his sight.

But there was not, it seemed, to be violence. At least not the hand-to-hand kind. The racing, crouching figure before him had come with a bodyguard.

As Benson leaped from the front door and crossed the porch in a single lithe stride, shots burst out from both ends of the house.

The Avenger's body jerked as two slugs hit him. They were stopped by his bulletproof undergarments, but the impact of a .45 bullet is very heavy. The rest of the shots missed their flickering target.

At the curb was a sedan that sagged on its tires in a way to indicate that it was armored. The fleeing figure ahead of The Avenger leaped into this. The car started away.

Out of its leg holster leaped the little special .22, Mike. It whispered twice as The Avenger raced toward the car. A bullet went into each rear tire; but, as Benson had thought, they were filled with petroleum jelly and immune to bullets. The car sped on.

A dozen men were running after Dick Benson, now,

shooting as they came. With so many, some one bullet would be bound, in a few seconds, to get him either in the head or the legs, where his celluglass garment did not extend to shield him from slugs.

Down the street, a little distance from where the sedan had been, were two other cars, used also by this gang when they came with their crippled, mad leader. Dick reached the first of these and sprang in.

Bullets ripped through windshield and windows. This was an ordinary stolen car, not bullet-proofed.

The Avenger slid out the other side and went back to the second car. White spots appeared on glass, but the slugs making them did not penetrate. This car was bullet-proof. He slammed into gear and rolled after the vanished sedan, with the men behind yelling their fury and fruitlessly emptying their guns at him.

In his made-up face, The Avenger's eyes were like glacial ice under a polar dawn. He had gotten clear of a death trap, but he had lost that ill-formed, crippled monster who had run screaming from him down Blake's hall.

However, there was a measure of icy satisfaction in Benson's pale, awesome eyes. The venture into the conference of the power barons had not been entirely without results, after all.

Smitty, at Marville according to his chief's orders, lurked in the woods around Plant 4 for half an hour before venturing to go in.

Benson had instructed him to look for a dead man, to start with the plant itself and work out, searching for murder.

The order was still utterly mysterious to Smitty; but he, as well as all the rest of the reckless little crime-fighting band, always obeyed The Avenger's orders to the letter, whether they seemed to make sense or not.

Start with the plant. Well, that was not as hard as it had sounded, the giant found.

Evidently, Grant Utilities Corp. had given up, temporarily at least, searching for the trouble at their glittering but useless Plant 4. There were no white-collared experts around, and no workmen. There was just one man, middle-aged, who was there as a watchman. Smitty confirmed that fact in his spying on the plant.

The big fellow went back along the path he had taken from his car, parked in a thicket a mile away. He came upon a spot he remembered, which would serve his purpose.

The spot was a low knoll, with bare space around it for forty or fifty yards, and dried, scrubby-looking brush on top of it. Smitty lit a match.

In a moment the brush was blazing, with smoke rising up from it. Actually, the knoll was so placed that fire could not spread over the bare spots to the woods themselves. But the thing, from a distance, would look like the beginning of a dangerous forest fire.

Smitty ran silently back to the plant. As he got near the gate he side-stepped while the middle-aged watchman tore past him to investigate the fire and put it out.

Smitty went on more leisurely, with the plant all his for at least fifteen minutes.

"Search for a dead man."

A corpse, whether produced by murder or by legitimate accident or disease, almost invariably is buried somewhere. So as Smitty searched, he kept his eyes directed downward.

He was looking for some section of flooring that seemed to have been recently disturbed. And over by the big switchboard, he found such a section.

There was a ragged strip, about a yard wide, in the cement floor from the board to No. 3 generator. It was easy to surmise what had made it: In checking the uncanny failure of the plant, somebody had ripped up the floor to expose the cables from generators to switchboard. Then new cement had been smoothed into place, leaving that slightly ragged strip over the trench.

There was a huge wrench nearby, a solid-looking six-foot spanner as heavy as a sledge hammer. Smitty picked that up.

Concrete hardens very quickly into usable firmness; but not for some time does it achieve its final flinty hardness. This was fresh enough to yield to the giant's colossal strength.

A dozen whistling blows with the hundred-pound spanner smashed the short strip into jagged fragments. Smitty pried them out and exposed the cinder blanket under the floor. This was scratched aside, too, a little dirt thrown up—

Smitty stared at the toe of a shoe. He touched it with the spanner. Its firmness indicated that there was a foot inside it.

Smitty worked fast. The thing was exposed in a few minutes. And then, shuddering a little, he examined it.

The corpse was that of a man. But of what man it was going to be difficult to ascertain because the torso was headless! The head had been raggedly cut off and taken somewhere else, since it was not in evidence in the exposed trench.

The man, before being killed, had been tortured in a manner to make the blood run cold. Evidences of the inhuman treatment were obvious on the headless body.

Smitty suddenly examined the throat as a rather unnatural thing caught his eyes. The throat muscles seemed a bit scrawnier, slightly withered, on the left side.

Hunt for a corpse, The Avenger had quietly directed. And by all that was mysterious, here was a corpse. Smitty felt the old awe of the man with the death-mask face and the pale, dreadful eyes well up in his vast chest.

A freshly murdered man. Well, that was only partly true, depending on what you called fresh. Smitty could see that this body had reposed in the cable trench for at least a month.

Off through a lofty window, he could see the smoke of the fire he had started fading down almost to nothingness as the watchman got it under control. Not much time left.

Smitty debated whether to take the grisly thing from under the floor along with him, shivered and decided against it, then edged it back into its impromptu grave.

With a broom from a near rack, he swept dirt over it, trod it down, then spread the cinders back in an even layer. The fragments of concrete, he didn't bother with. There was no disguising the way the fresh strip of cement had been ripped up. The watchman would have to find it and wonder why it had been done in his short absence. Perhaps he would dig himself and find the body. In any event, Smitty's quest had been successful.

A man showing signs of having been tortured to death, with the head removed to make identification impossible, buried under the floor of Plant 4. Just where did *that* enter into this mad, tremendous affair of power blackouts and insane cripples?

Smitty was blessed if he knew.

CHAPTER XIII

Enter The Feds

The first power shut-off, lasting only a few seconds, had not been much commented on. The second one, lasting for minutes, had been commented on widely. And the comments were growing. In fact, they were mounting into a sort of continental hysteria that embraced Canada as well as the United States.

All power blanked out for over a quarter of an hour! *All* power—airplane and automobile and motorboat systems as well as great power generators! It was as horrible in its implications as it was incredible.

There were several wild theories to account for the thing. The most commonly held was that a hostile foreign power had done it as an experiment, perhaps to prove to its military staff that it could be done, perhaps as a terrifying groundwork for some piratical military demand to be made in the near future.

A war measure! The United States and Canada perhaps to be drawn at last, directly, into war on their own soil!

Several scores of war-weary refugees, who had fled to America in a last, desperate effort to escape Mars' madness, became hysterical and committed suicide, utterly unable to face once more the inhumanities of modern warfare.

Hundreds of thousands of people fled to the open country and became burdens there on the local country people. The stock and bond markets dropped so fast that the exchanges had to be closed.

The whole natural life of the continent was in danger of being dislocated; so the government, naturally, stepped in, and stepped in hard.

Half the entire staff of Federal officers was turned over to the task of solving the mystery of the power failure. And leading this half, personally, was Paul Edward Arnold.

Arnold turned his full attention on the power failure, and in a short time he began getting little loose ends to tie together.

It started with an anonymous tip.

His phone rang and a man's voice, obviously disguised, said:

"In the last power failure a man named Richard Benson was present at the Portland, Maine, radio tower. Also, at about the same time, Richard Benson phoned a Los Angeles radio station, probably to give orders."

"What?" snapped Arnold, having instantly set in motion the dictaphone that recorded all telephone conversations. "What was that about Benson? And who are you?"

The man at the other end seemed to know exactly why Arnold asked for a repetition. Arnold was stalling till an officer could locate that telephone and race to it. So he didn't bite.

"Also," the disguised voice went on, "Richard Benson

has been active around Marville, Ohio, where a power plant has been mysteriously unable to generate power since its completion."

There was a click. The phone had been hung up. And long before anyone could get to it, the speaker would be gone.

Arnold hated anonymous tips. All law officers do. But all officers work on them, just the same. They can't afford to ignore what may be a wide-open lead given by a disgruntled crook or by some private citizen afraid to let his name become known because of possible criminal revenge.

So Arnold got his little loose ends.

A radio tower in Portland and another in Los Angeles that had all power tubes blown during the blackout and also had showed signs of fusing, intense heat. A power plant that wouldn't run, in Ohio, which had been made useless a few weeks before the midnight failure.

And Richard Benson *had* been present in all of this.

Arnold went through a process of reasoning as brilliant as it was erroneous.

The man known as The Avenger was the world's best electrical engineer, he had heard. If anyone could perform the miracle of stopping power plants, it would be Benson.

The Avenger had helped the government in several important cases; he was known to every high official. Yet, in the last analysis no one knew anything *about* him. He was essentially a man of mystery.

And he had been mixed up in this even before the government asked him to work on it. Arnold checked and found that out.

However, though circumstantial evidence pointed strongly at Benson, Arnold didn't make up his mind. He knew The Avenger had trusted him. Arnold was a fair man, and circumstantial evidence was not enough.

It remained for the sworn statement of a man whose name was known from coast to coast to burst like a bombshell in Arnold's office and damn Benson irrevocably.

The man was Pierpont Ryan, who had taken a plane to Washington from Cleveland.

He told of the secret meeting at Blake's home and of a madman's demand for five million dollars on threat of permanently shutting off America's power.

"Said his name was Nevlo," barked Ryan. Arnold nodded. His investigations had already brought Nevlo into the picture so that he knew the discharged engineer's background. "But then a second Nevlo came in just in time to spoil the game of the first."

He told all about that, too, and Arnold's face went more white and grim with each word.

"That first man," concluded Ryan, jaw set like rock, "was a fellow named Benson. I could see that, later. I know Benson well; I was licked by him in a couple of South American power deals years ago. As he ran down the hall I saw him reach to his eyes to take off little lenses that had made them black. Benson's eyes are almost white, you know. Only one man has those colorless, flaring eyes—Richard Benson. Yes, no doubt of it, it was Benson."

"And he demanded five million?" said Arnold, lips thin.

"Yes. The second man—Nevlo, or whoever he was—evidently knew a little of Benson's plan and tried to horn in. But—the man who made the *real* extortion demand was Benson!"

No disputing the word of a magnate like Ryan. He was a well-known character, and one against whom no shadow had ever fallen. This was the bombshell. Richard Benson, the only man in America logically capable of the power shut-off, had actually been the one who did it. For five million dollars—

"But he's rich," mused Arnold aloud. "Tremendously rich—"

"Few men are rich enough not to want five million dollars cash in a lump," snapped Ryan.

Arnold nodded. That was unfortunately true. After Ryan left, he called his best ten men into his office.

"We're going after Benson," he said, after telling what had gone before.

Of the ten crack Federal officers, seven had seen The Avenger personally and the other three had heard volumes about him. The oldest man among them licked lips that had suddenly gone dry.

"After *Benson*?"

"Yes!"

"I'd rather go after the United States army."

Arnold's face grew grimmer yet.

"I know as well as you do what kind of a man he is. If he's innocent, he ought to come with any of you for questioning readily enough. But if he shows the slightest sign of resistance—well, we'll have to have him, dead or alive. This thing is too huge, too terrible, to take any chances with."

Next day, after this secret talk in Arnold's world-famous office, the man talked about landed in Cleveland. With Dick Benson was Janet Weems.

Janet's condition had been described by Benson—a great psychiatrist himself—as almost certainly temporary, induced by great nervous strain. It had proved to be a true diagnosis. Shortly after being rescued from the house on Vermont Avenue in Portland, she had snapped out of it.

She had told Benson what had thrown her into the state of delirium. She had then drawn for him the diagram Bill Burton had wanted her to give him with the needles.

At sight of the diagram, showing what seemed a large needle with a root going under a wavy line and with shorter lines coming from its tip but not quite meeting it, The Avenger's eyes had glittered.

The glitter in his awesome eyes told that he already

knew about all there was to be known about this affair, but was not yet ready for final action.

There would have to be a little more investigation first. So he was in Cleveland on the matter, now, with Janet.

"Must you go to the spot where Bill Burton's car—exploded?" said Janet with a shudder.

"I'm afraid we must," The Avenger said in his quiet but vibrant voice.

"But that was days ago," pointed out Janet. "Nothing could be learned there, now."

"No trail is so cold," said Dick, "but what some fact may be turned up if it is followed. I know it's painful to you, but we must investigate."

So they went to the spot around the corner from the obscure hotel where Janet had hidden. And Janet reconstructed the scene for Benson.

Car there. Parked cars down farther. Janet here. Tremendous blast, rolling clouds of smoke—

The Avenger stepped into the store nearest the spot where Burton's car had been demolished. The storekeeper said that he had been there when the blast took place. He had looked out of his show window a moment later. What had happened to the man in the car, he did not know. Apparently he had been blown to bits. The storeowner did not remember reading in the papers anything about a body.

Benson's pale, deadly eyes were quite as infallible as they looked. They were like twin diamond drills that could pierce through and through any pretense. Those colorless eyes saw evasion and fright behind the storekeeper's smooth statements.

"From all accounts," said Benson, "there was a lot of heavy black smoke around the car, hiding it, just after the explosion."

The Avenger's voice had changed. The change was

subtle, but distinct enough for Janet Weems to catch it. She stared quickly at his calm face.

The store-owner said, "Yes, there was a lot of smoke."

"Enough, perhaps," Benson went on in that level, monotonous, hypnotic tone, "to hide movements of anyone near the car?"

The storekeeper seemed to be going through a curious, dazed struggle as he stared into the pale, awesome eyes. He obviously tried to look away from them—and obviously could not do so. Janet Weems stared breathlessly as she realized what was happening. This man beside her, in a matter of seconds and with no instruments but his quiet, compelling voice and brilliant, colorless eyes, was hypnotizing the man.

"I suppose such movements could have been hidden by the smoke," said the storekeeper in a curious, smothered tone.

"Then if someone had reached in and taken the body from the wreckage of the car, the people nearby might not have seen it? But you could have seen it, close as this window is to the spot."

"Yes, I could have seen it," said the storekeeper, tone becoming mechanical.

"Now," commanded The Avenger, "you will tell me just what you *did* see?"

"The man in the car was not killed," said the store-owner. "I saw him reel from the car. Most of his clothes had been torn or burned off. He was out on his feet and hadn't the least idea what he was doing. But he was alive."

"Oh, thank Heaven!" cried Janet.

She stopped immediately, aware that a sharp exclamation might undo what The Avenger had accomplished. The man stirred a little, but couldn't escape the pale eyes.

"So by some freak of explosion, the man did not get killed when his car was blown up," nodded Benson. "All right, what happened then?"

"The nearest of the cars parked down the street had

two men in it," said the storekeeper. "I think they, and I, were the only ones who saw the man get out of the car. They came running into the smoke. They looked as if not believing what their eyes told them. It seemed so impossible that any living thing could be spared by the blast."

"Then?"

"They got the man from the car down to their own machine and drove away."

"You seem to have observed everything minutely."

"I did."

"Then perhaps you can tell us something identifying about their car. Appearance, license number, something of that nature."

"I can. There was a banner tied on their rear bumper. They could not have noticed that, of course, or it would have been ripped off long ago. The banner read: 'Marville Natural Caves.' As the two men went back to the car with the dazed man, one saw the banner and jerked it off and put it in his pocket. But I had seen it by then."

Benson turned deliberately from the man, releasing him from the intangible chains forged by his brilliant, pale eyes.

"Thank you for the information," he said, in a different, harder tone.

The man blinked, then started a little.

"I suppose," said The Avenger, turning back, "you kept this information to yourself for fear of gang reprisals."

"Yes, I did," said the man. "Say—what did I tell you, anyway?"

"Quite a bit. For which, again, thanks."

The Avenger went out with Janet. On the street, he looked at her.

"Banners? Caves?"

"There is a quite large cave formation several miles out of Marville," explained Janet. "The local chamber of commerce has been trying for a long time to make it a tourist attraction. They advertise it once in a while, and they have a shell-shocked World War veteran there for a few dollars a week to act as guide. Only about a dozen tourists a week come there. But the guide is zealous; he ties a banner to every rear bumper, as he was ordered. He did it this time—to a gangster car."

"We go south to Marville," said The Avenger.

Behind them, the store-owner was cursing himself for somehow having told a thing he had resolved never to breathe to a soul. Gang murder! He knew what sometimes happened to innocent bystanders who informed on phases of gang wars.

But having told once, he saw no reason not to tell again when, about an hour later, several men came in and asked about the questions the man with the dead face had asked. The men were special Federal investigators, headed by P. Edward Arnold, himself.

"Gone to Marville, eh?" repeated Arnold. "We'll get him there."

In the government car, which was armored like a rolling fortress, one of his men said, "You still want him—dead or alive?"

Arnold nodded, face regretful but eyes grim. He had thought a lot of Richard Benson. But the evidence against him, among which was a witnessed attempt at extortion, was too conclusive.

"If we say we want to take him in for questioning," his man pointed out, "he may say he simply can't be delayed now because he is on the edge of making important discoveries."

Arnold nodded to that, too. "Yes, that would be the most logical way to try to stall. But it can't be allowed. He surrenders instantly, or you shoot him down. Sorry, but that's the way it has to be. The welfare of our nation depends on it."

CHAPTER XIV

Daggers Of Death!

In our broad land there are dozens of cavern systems almost rivaling the famous natural caves of Kentucky. Not quite as extensive as the Mammoth Caves, they are yet vast underground labyrinths filled with natural beauty —and with death for the unwary one who goes too far from an exit and loses his way.

In nearly every case the businessmen of the nearest town try to attract tourists to their caves. But it is hard to make a dent in the prevailing public apathy to things subterranean.

It was so in this case. Janet's guess that a dozen tourists a week came to the Marville Natural Caves was probably overly generous. And the few who did come never went beyond the first huge cave, because there was a bottomless rift between that and the next one. And the "guide" didn't know of any other entrances.

That guide, by the way, The Avenger and Janet found

as they got to the entrance of the caves, would never tie any more banners to rear bumpers. He was dead!

He lay just inside the cave mouth with his throat slashed from ear to ear.

Janet exclaimed in pity, "Poor fellow. He wasn't quite right from his shell shock. It was like killing a child—"

"Even a child can see too much to be allowed to live," Dick said quietly.

"But what on earth could this poor man have seen?"

"Let's go on farther," suggested Benson, "and see if we can find out."

They went into the cave. They had covered at least four hundred yards and gone around half a hundred spectacularly fantastic and beautiful stalagmites, before they reached the end of the trail. The end, at least, as far as Janet knew.

This was a rift in solid rock that was about fifty feet across, as Dick's powerful little flash revealed. And it went straight down to depths out of reach of the flashlight's beam.

"There's water down there," said Benson.

"Is there?" Janet had thought she had fine ears, but she couldn't hear any water.

"Yes. An underground stream. And it must flow to the south, since all the land here slopes that way. We can go back out, find the stream, and perhaps get into the rest of the cavern system along it."

"Why go into them?"

"Because," said Benson, "there is some mystery about the Marville Caves that we want to find out about. There is plainly no mystery about this big, well-known entrance cave, so it must lie in the others."

"You'll have a hard time finding the stream as it comes above ground," said Janet pessimistically. "You see, there are a dozen little creeks outside here. I know, I used to play in most of them when I was a little girl, building dams and going wading. It will be next to impossible to decide which of them is the stream down there."

"It shouldn't be too hard," said Benson, voice calm almost to the point of indifference.

The Avenger wore a vest that had more little pockets in it than ten ordinary vests. He dipped into one of the pockets now and drew out a capsule about the size of an olive. This he dropped into the underground watery depths.

Janet looked puzzled.

"The shell of the capsule," said Benson, "will melt in a moment or two in the water. It will release a powerful dye. The dye will turn the water red, like blood, for many yards around. We'll go outside, now, and search for the stream that is reddish in color."

They returned to the entrance of the main cave. And Janet screamed sharply.

The body of the guide was no longer there!

The Avenger said nothing. He had been certain enough before that a lot of activity was taking place in this cave system. He needed nothing like the removal of the murdered man to prove it to him.

They went out. The fourth stream to the east, gushing from the side of the chain of hills forming the roof of the cavern system, was distinctly reddish in color.

They found the spot where the water came from the hillside. There was something like a jungle of trees and undergrowth around the spot, lush plants that flourished in the continual moisture. As if by instinct, The Avenger cut one extra-thick bush to the ground with Ike.

And a hole was revealed above the icy flow.

The hole was small, but by bending double he and Janet could get through it, wading up to their knees in the water.

"I'd heard there were other entrances to the caves," said Janet in a low tone. "But even the oldest residents around here didn't seem to know where they were."

"*Ssh!*" said Benson instantly.

They were in a small tunnel that was rapidly swelling into a big one. Up this long funnel, sound went tripping, doing odd magnifying things. Even The Avenger hadn't foreseen how odd.

His sibilant warning preceded them like an army of ghosts, with the near ones roaring and the far ones whispering.

"*SSH!*"
"*Ssh!*"
"*Ssh—*"
"*Sss—*"

Benson's flash lit a path for them like the headlight of a tiny locomotive. They went as fast as they could. If anyone were ahead of them, the echoing sound must have been a warning. Then, suddenly, the tunnel veered right and upward and left the stream. They climbed the incline to a point where, on their left, a deep chasm yawned.

Across the chasm was the main cave which they had entered first.

They turned away from the chasm and went back into unguessable depths.

"The caves are like a chain of beads," said Janet in a whisper.

They were. Like beads strung on a thread, the thread being a rift like a corridor, leading into and out of first one and then another.

But the rift soon forked.

"Now what?" whispered Janet. "Right, or left?"

There was a sound to their left, and the words: "Stay where you are and drop that light!"

The Avenger moved with the uncanny swiftness of which he was capable. Janet found herself suddenly in the right-hand fork as Benson lifted her and leaped with her. The flash went out. They had evaded the unseen foe.

There was a roar and a dreadful trembling of the solid

rock on which they stood. And down from the low-hanging roof, over the narrow bottleneck through which they had leaped, came tons of stone. It completely blocked their way back out.

Somebody laughed out there, and then a gun roared!

Fergus MacMurdie yawned and stretched.

He had had orders to follow the chief and Janet Weems in another plane and watch Blake's house. So he had come; and he had been watching, for nearly five hours, lying cramped behind a bush in the rear yard of the Blake estate.

He had seen nothing there, and had about concluded that for once Muster Benson was off on a cold scent. Then he saw the servants leave the place. They were looking contented enough, and it appeared that they had been unexpectedly given an evening off. So Mac regained his first alert watchfulness.

A big town car drew up in front of the place.

The front door was out of Mac's range of vision, so he went, like an Indian from bush to bush, to the side where he could see it. And he got there just in time to see a remarkable figure being smuggled out the front door and into the town car.

The figure was like that of a gorilla, with long arms and a crouching walk that came near to dragging the creature's knuckles on the ground.

"Nevlo!" Mac whispered to himself between set teeth. "The skurlie! 'Tis some hold he's got over Blake that he can make the mon shelter him in his home and drive him around in his town car!"

The Scot didn't have much time for reflections. The town car swirled off in a hurry, and Mac could barely get to his own rented coupé down the line in time to pick up the trail before Blake's glittering machine faded from sight completely.

It went south of Marville.

Mac followed, far behind, through the little town and out into open country. It was not to the power plant they were going. Mac knew that. In fact, it seemed as if they weren't going anywhere, because the town car dumped the misshapen gorilla in open country just south of a line of low hills and then rolled back toward Marville as if the devil were after it.

Mac bit his lips in indecision as to which to follow, and decided that Nevlo was the more important man to trail. He went after the monstrosity who had been a fine engineer.

Suddenly, along a creek bank, Nevlo seemed to disappear.

It was night, now, but not *that* dark. The Scot found the explanation in a moment. There was a hole out of which the creek was gushing. Beside the hole there was a thick stub where a shielding bush had recently been cut away.

A concealed hole in the ground. This must have been where Nevlo went.

Mac crowded himself through the hole and along the path The Avenger had taken. He followed Nevlo by sound, now, ears tuned to the drag of those uneven, crippled footsteps.

Up an incline, to the right—

The Scot heard the sound of a shot ahead, a roaring report magnified many times, like a snare drum. He saw the gorilla form ahead—outlined in the backwash of a flash he held—start to run. And Mac ran, too.

He went through caves like beads on the chain of the crude tunnel they were in. Ahead of him, Nevlo stopped. There was a man there, with a rifle. The man was beside a sort of breastworks formed of recently fallen rock.

Between the rock and the roof was a two-foot hole. As Mac neared Nevlo and the man with the gun, he saw the latter, grinning, thrust the rifle through the opening, aim, and fire!

From beyond the barricade Mac heard a heavy, booming crash. Then he could see into the cave a little by the aid of a flashlight which the grinning marksman had strapped to his rifle barrel.

Mac felt such rage fill him as even the bitter Scot seldom experienced.

In there were two people, trapped by the rock slide. Over their heads hung dozens of ponderous stalactites, huge icicle-like incrustations. The man with the gun had been amusing himself by firing at the stalactites over the heads of the two, sending them crashing down like great daggers of death.

One of the massive things was bound to catch the two and crush them. Quite an amusing game.

Then a strange thing happened. With this last shot, the marksman hadn't bothered to get his head out of range of the opening when he turned. Probably he had decided some time ago that his two victims were helpless and unarmed. But it seemed they were not so helpless.

There was a subdued little *spat*; a gash appeared on the exact top of the marksman's skull, and he fell. There was a foolish look on his unconscious face, marred a bit by a trickle of blood from the gash.

"*Whoosh!*" breathed Mac. "Only one gun could do that, in the hands of one man—the chief."

So the Scot leaped for the remaining enemy, Nevlo!

Mac had fists, as has been said, like bone mallets. They were about as good a weapon as anyone could own, aside from actual firearms. They had seldom let him down.

But they did so now.

He got a right and left square in the hideous face of the monstrosity, who had whirled, snarling, to confront the man who had tiptoed behind him from the secret entrance. And the two blows didn't stop Nevlo at all.

Nevlo didn't attempt to hit back. He wound his gorilla arms around Mac's sinewy body, pinning the Scot's arms to his sides, and squeezed!

Mac gasped in that mighty bear hug. He tried to get loose and couldn't. He heard a roaring in his ears, and felt his ribs cracking!

The terrible pressure, after how long a period he couldn't even guess, was relieved. He fell, as the arms uncoiled, and lay gasping on the rock floor.

The monster was roaring in pain, with the roars getting more suffocated every second. And Mac saw why.

From the opening between rock barricade and roof a steely arm was thrust. At the end of the arm was a hand, slim, not large, with muscles like little wire cables standing out on it.

Dick Benson's hand. And it was clamped over the back of Nevlo's neck, in the dreadful nerve pressure that could put a man out in a minute, kill him in two.

Had Benson been in the clear instead of straining to reach from a distance, his gorilla-like opponent probably never could have done it. As it was, Nevlo managed to jerk loose, the only person who had ever broken that hold.

Still roaring with pain and rage, he raced back past Mac and down the tunnel.

Mac got to the opening when Benson had half finished making it large enough for him and Janet Weems to get out.

"*Whoosh!*" said the Scot, feeling tenderly at his ribs. "I thought it was ye I'd rescue, Muster Benson. But it looks like ye rescued me."

The three of them went back down the tunnel toward the stream exit. Janet trembled a little, but was game. They crawled out into the open night, Benson first. And up from the bushes rose a dozen men.

"Put your hands up, Benson," came a voice. "You are

under arrest. Don't try anything, because if you do we'll shoot at once. And believe me, I'd rather not have to do that."

The Avenger's hands were up a little way above his head. Those marvelous, pale eyes of his had identified the speaker even in the darkness and had told him that the threat was deadly in its sincerity.

Benson had a lot of things he wanted to do immediately. He simply could not allow himself to be delayed like this. But he couldn't afford to die, either.

Paul Edward Arnold, himself, stooped and took Mike and Ike warily from their leg holsters; Arnold was one of the few who knew the existence and location of those two little weapons used with such deadly effectiveness by The Avenger.

CHAPTER XV

Prison Walls

The Marville jail was the last word in strength and efficiency. The bars were of case-hardened steel, nearly two inches thick. The walls were of brick, reinforced throughout. Floors were of cement. The locks might have baffled Houdini.

Even the sheriff's office, a big room in the rear of the building, was of that type of construction. In that rear room, a lot of prisoners were intensively questioned, and the sheriff didn't want to risk jailbreaks by them or their friends.

Dick Benson was back in that rear room, now.

He had been taken to a cell by Arnold, after quite a talk between the two men, a talk that had helped The Avenger not at all.

"Of course I've been in the thick of this," said Benson calmly. "The government asked me to investigate, didn't it?"

"The government," said Arnold bleakly, "didn't ask

you to try to extort five million dollars from a bunch of utilities men."

"I was playing a part," retorted Benson. "I went through an act, to see if I could confirm a suspicion of mine. And I did confirm it."

"Just what did you find out?" Arnold inquired icily.

The Avenger had looked around at half a dozen Federal men, the Marville sheriff, and several burly deputies.

Sheriff and Federal men were probably above suspicion. But The Avenger couldn't be sure of the deputies. He dared not take chances with them in an affair of such magnitude.

"It is too soon," he said evenly to Arnold, "to tell what I have discovered to date."

"I'm afraid you're going to have to tell. If not here, then in Washington. There is a through train at four-thirty in the morning. I am arranging to have that stop at Marville. We will take you to Washington on it."

"You'll be making a serious mistake to delay me like that," said The Avenger, pale eyes like ice in moonlight.

"I'll have to take that chance," shrugged Arnold. "Personally, I think you're guilty as hell. But you'll be given every chance to disprove your guilt, in the next few days in Washington."

Benson's eyes had glittered like little agates. In a few more days this gigantic crime plot would be successfully concluded, with a tremendous blackmail sum gathered by the archcrook and all evidence to convict him carefully destroyed. He simply could not give up the time Arnold demanded.

But he had saved his breath at the look in Arnold's face.

Arnold and his men had left, after seeing Benson locked in the jail's stoutest cell. But hardly had the special government men left when the Marville sheriff led Benson out of that cell and to his rear room.

The sheriff was a good officer, but he had a desire for publicity of the right sort. And here was a gorgeous chance.

The power plot was the biggest thing in the crime history of the country. It had the nation so excited it could scarcely sleep nights. The man who cracked it would be the nation's hero.

And the sheriff saw no reason why he shouldn't be that man.

If this fellow with the colorless eyes really knew something, he should be forced to tell it; then the sheriff would carry on from there.

There were three deputies with him when he herded Benson into the rear room. Benson, hands cuffed behind him, stood for a moment and faced the four. And for a second even the sheriff had his doubts.

This man was not large. Any one of the four of them was inches taller and pounds heavier. He seemed helpless with the handcuffs binding him. Yet there was something distinctly disquieting about the way he stood there.

"Sit down!" barked the sheriff, indicating a straight-backed kitchen chair.

Benson calmly sat down.

"I shall, of course, tell you nothing, sheriff," he said, with no more emotion in his vibrant voice than in his calm face.

"You'll talk," said the sheriff. "You can start by telling me where Nevlo is and how you get into them caves near where Arnold picked you up."

The Avenger said nothing. He wouldn't have answered in any case. But even if he had felt like speaking, he would have held off because he was listening hard to something.

Something out in the night.

The night was unseasonably warm, so the side window of the rear room was open. The thick bars set in solid steel casements were revealed. And from out there, just barely to be heard even by The Avenger's fine ears was a *pop-popping* roar like that of an airplane just ready to take off.

Only, of course, the airplane would have had to be taking off from one of the city streets, since there was no airport that near.

"Come on," said the sheriff, filled with visions of being a national hero. "Where's Nevlo?"

The muffled booming of a heavy motor sounded nearer. The sheriff and deputies could hear it now, too. One of the deputies raised an eyebrow.

"That's a big truck," he commented.

"Probably one of them twenty-ton trailer outfits from Akron," said another. "So what? We don't care about trucks."

The big motor changed tune as it suddenly idled, out there in the night. Perhaps the driver had stopped for a cup of coffee.

There was the faintest of sounds from outside the open window.

The Avenger had been forced to sit down with his hands behind his back. Those hands now gripped the uprights of the heavy, plain chairback. He pulled a little. His slim fingers went whiter than normal with strain.

There was a thin screaming sound of wood strained beyond endurance. Then The Avenger dropped the back of the chair on the floor behind him. He had plucked it out of its glued and doweled holes as easily as if the two uprights had been two stalks of asparagus.

"For—" began one of the deputies in a whisper. But he stopped with the first word, mouth open. Not a man of them could have duplicated that feat, even with unbound hands and standing upright to brace knees and shoulders and back for the pull.

The Avenger's eyes, like stainless-steel chips, regarded them all calmly. He had not plucked the back out of the seat simply to show off. He had done it to rivet their attention to him for a moment. And for an excellent reason.

He didn't want any of them glancing at the window for a while.

Around the two central bars, an instant before, had been cautiously placed two thick steel hooks. From the hooks went one-inch steel cable.

"Maybe," said one of the deputies, staring uneasily at the chairback lying on the floor, "we better take this guy back to his cell and wait for Arnold to—"

The Avenger stood up. Hands behind him, he raised the remnant of the chair as he got to his feet. His left hand moved a little, and calmly and easily a rung broke out with a report like that of a pistol shot.

Again he had done it to keep the men's eyes away from the window and to keep their ears from hearing a slight noise of the hooks over the bars, a noise caused by the tightening of the cable behind the hooks.

"We're not waiting for Arnold!" snapped the sheriff. "Answer my question, Benson—What're you nuzzling the lapel of your coat for?"

The sheriff got the answer to that, an instant later, with no word from The Avenger.

"Hey!" said one of the deputies. "I feel kinda funny—"

With the last word, he sagged toward the floor. And the other three men slumped floorward, too. While from a tiny vial dropped, uncorked, just inside the open window, came the last of almost colorless fumes.

Out there, a flashlight blinked twice. With the signal, from down the street, came the roar of that big motor as it stopped idling and went to work.

The cable behind the heavy hooks tightened and thrummed like a fishline with a tarpon on it. And the bars came out of the wall. So did the steel casement and some of the surrounding bricks.

In through the jagged opening stepped Fergus Mac-Murdie. He kept the lapel of his coat over his nostrils, as did The Avenger, to exclude the little vial's fumes, a paralyzing gas.

"All right, Muster Benson?" said the Scot.

"All right, Mac," said Benson.

His handcuffs dropped on the floor behind him. There were raw spots on his steely wrists, but that was all. Few handcuffs could hold The Avenger.

He went to the sheriff's desk and retrieved the two weapons he had seen dropped in the top drawer. Mike and Ike. Then he and Mac went to the jagged hole where a window had been, leaving three deputies and a sheriff lying fast asleep on the floor beside them.

Down the street, Smitty waved cheerfully. The giant had "borrowed" a huge caterpillar tractor from a road outfit, which had been left standing at a new road on the town's outskirts, ready for tomorrow's work. With the tractor, he had borrowed the big hooks and a hundred yards of steel cable.

The tractor had been the truck-and-trailer outfit idly guessed at by the deputy.

The three men went to the car Mac had left three blocks away. Josh Newton grinned toothily from the wheel.

"Marville Caves, Josh," said Benson.

They went past the cave entrance, to the south-hill slope where the creek gushed from the side of the range. But they never quite reached that entrance.

Walking noiselessly through the night from the distant spot where Josh had stopped the car, they halted abruptly as all four saw the same thing.

Two men were running along the dark skyline some yards to their left.

The four sprang toward them. The one in front was being hotly pursued by the one in the rear and was obviously in distress.

As they got closer, they could see them more plainly.

The one in front seemed like a living scarecrow, thin, weak, in rags. The one in the rear looked more like a gorilla than a man, and in his right hand was clutched a murderous club.

The figure in the rear saw the approaching four first.

"Nevlo!" Smitty's voice cracked out.

In answer there was a hoarse yell of anger and defiance. And then the figure wasn't there any more. It had disappeared as if by magic—disappeared downward, as though sinking into the solid earth.

The man who had been chased now stumbled and fell. He lay where he had fallen, panting hard.

CHAPTER XVI

Into The Earth

Smitty gently helped the man to his feet.

At close range, he looked more than ever like a scarecrow. He was emaciated, and his rags covered his body even more scantily than at first realized. On the exposed areas of skin were the flat, terrible marks of recent burning.

"He looks scared out of his hide!" said Mac, sympathetically.

The man certainly did. His eyes were dazed with fear. They were blank, almost unseeing, too. He looked like a witless yokel who had been terrified by a ghost in a graveyard.

"Needles," he croaked. He looked into first one and then another of the four faces close to him. Then his gaze centered on The Avenger, as if, even in his delirium, he recognized authority.

"Benson. Needles. Get to Benson with the needles with roots."

"What in the worrrld—" burred Mac.

"Shut up!" snapped Smitty. "Listen. Don't you get it? This is Burton, the engineer put in charge of Plant 4. He got those burns when his car blew up."

"Needles," mumbled Burton, his eyes wild but blank. "Some chemical. Can't figure out what. Some chemical. Electrical vacuum."

Benson looked hard into the dazed, staring eyes.

"He won't be able to answer questions coherently tonight, at least," he said. "Josh, take him back to Cleveland. Hide him out there."

The last thing Benson and Mac and Smitty heard as Josh led Burton away was the murmur from the sick man's slack lips:

"Some kind of chemical . . ."

The Avenger went forward into the night. He stared downward carefully as he advanced.

He was searching for the spot where the gorilla form had disappeared. Though he knew that "disappeared" was not the word for it. Material substances don't do that very easily.

Smitty and Mac were close behind him. They exclaimed at the thing that finally stopped their chief.

There was a smooth, round hole in the ground at the point where the monster had disappeared. Their flashlights showed that it slanted a little; it did not go straight down. It was almost as smooth and symmetrical as a mail chute.

"A mail chute to hell, though," said Mac dourly.

To one side of the hole was a wooden cover, like a manhole cover. On this was a foot of earth topped by sod, hiding the hole from prying eyes.

Benson lowered himself into the hole. Suspended by his elbows he looked up at Mac and Smitty.

"I'll call out when I get to the bottom," he said. "If I don't call, go back and get the government men."

He dropped.

Mac and Smitty waited on their haunches beside the grim-looking chute. And no sound came up out of the hole. Mac stared at Smitty, then put his face close to earth so that his voice wouldn't be heard at a distance.

"Muster Benson!"

There was no answer. Mac moistened lips gone suddenly dry.

"*Chief!*"

There was no sound from the hole in the earth.

"I'm goin' afterrr him," said Mac determinedly.

Smitty clutched his arm. "He said to get Arnold and his men if he didn't call—"

"That'd take too much time."

Mac dropped out of sight, too. And Smitty waited anxiously in the night.

No call.

The giant looked over the fields. Then he eyed the hole. He decided promptly that for once The Avenger's orders were to be disobeyed. By the time he could get in touch with Arnold, Dick and Mac would have been murdered a dozen times down there.

If, indeed, they weren't both dead already!

Smitty squeezed his great body into the hole, then let go the sides.

He began to slide downward.

Faster and faster he went, slanting up a little, dropping a little more steeply, turning a bit. The thing was more than ever like a mail chute, in its smooth turnings and twistings.

Smitty couldn't move his massive arms in the chute enough to brake his fall. But he could stare down past his own descending bulk, a little, enough to see light, which grew as he fell.

Then he was at the end of the thing so suddenly that a grunt was forced from his lips as he thudded onto the small of his back and sprawled like an overturned crab.

From that undignified and helpless angle, he stared up

and saw the man who looked and walked like a gorilla. The man still had his club in his misshapen hands. The club was lifted high, and on the man's lips was a humorless grin of anticipation.

Smitty managed to get one hamlike hand up a little, but that was the only move he could make in his own defense.

The club whistled down!

Smitty was sitting upright, in a most awkward and uncomfortable position. But he couldn't seem to do anything about it. When he tried to twist arms or legs to attain a new position, legs and arms refused to work.

He opened his eyes. At first all he saw was a yellow glow that waxed and waned with his heartbeats and in time with pain throbs that also occurred with each beat of his heart.

Incidentally, his heart seemed to be beating in his head instead of his chest and seemed to be about the size of an accordion, which someone was opening and shutting.

He got his eyes to functioning again.

He was in a cave about thirty by thirty feet, with a roof dipping down to about eight feet from the roughrock floor. The cave was lighted by a candle that was stuck in the neck of a bottle in one corner. The candle guttered and threw weird shadows around the place.

Then Smitty saw Mac and Dick.

The two of them sat on an oil drum apiece. At least, they looked like oil drums. They were the same size, of rolled steel, with reinforcing ridges around their centers.

Dick and Mac were bound like a couple of mummies and sat with their backs against the wall. That was his own position, Smitty realized. And he was bound, too, which was why he couldn't shift out of his awkward posture.

The Avenger's pale, deadly eyes were open. They

were calmly surveying the cavern. Smitty saw them rest for an appreciable instant on the ceiling.

He looked that way, too.

Down the center of the rock roof ran a thick, bare copper wire or bar. It was about a half-inch in diameter and looked like a lightning conductor. At the end, it split into three. One length was attached to the drum on which Benson sat. Another went to Mac's uncomfortable throne. The third passed out of Smitty's sight under his knees, so he guessed that it was similarly connected with his drum.

The far end of the copper conduit couldn't be seen. The thing went out the low entrance of the cave and off to some other point.

Mac moaned and opened his eyes. He snapped out of it a little faster than Smitty had. He stared at Benson, tried to move, and said, "*Uggh!*"

"Exactly," said Smitty.

The Avenger's pale eyes rested on Smitty's moonface, and the giant found it hard to meet that clear, colorless gaze.

"I believe you two were to have gone to get Arnold if I didn't call out," said Benson.

"I—" said Smitty. "We—"

Mac said thickly, "We didn't want to take all that time when ye might be in the process of bein' murrrdered, Muster Benson."

"Besides," said Smitty, "you're always facing risks that you don't want the rest of us to take. We thought maybe you were just trying to make us leave a tight spot."

The pale, infallible eyes passed from their faces, much to the relief of both. An order had been given. Out of sheer loyalty, it had been disobeyed. There was no use discussing it further.

The Avenger stared again at the thick copper cable

that came from somewhere outside the cavern and ended with the three steel drums.

"What is all this contraption, Muster Benson?" Mac asked, blinking his bleak blue eyes.

Smitty knew why he was blinking, because he was doing the same thing. The light from the candle, feeble as it was, exaggerated the ache left from the sock on the head he had received at the foot of the chute. It looked, however, as though the light wasn't going to plague them much longer. The candle was a mere stub in the bottleneck. It would breathe its last any minute now, and then leave them in darkness.

Smitty vastly preferred the ache to the prospective darkness!

"This contraption," Dick said quietly, echoing the Scot's word for it, "contains the secret of the power blackout, Mac. A little thing discovered by Nevlo. It is probably the apparatus that keeps Plant 4 from generating power. And it was a similar arrangement, on a larger scale, that blanked out the power of a continent."

"*Whoosh!*" said the Scot. "Then we've finally tracked it down!" Which disregarded somewhat the fact that they had fallen into it, rather than done any tracking.

It was usually the part of MacMurdie to croak dismally of sure failure. Smitty took the role himself, this time.

"Sure," he said, "we've tracked it down. So what? We can't do anything about it."

"Oh, we'll get out of this mess," said Mac. For it was another of his strange characteristics that when things seemed blackest he invariably shed his pessimism and became as optimistic as a bird with a couple of worms.

Smitty stared at the cable.

"The secret of the power failures, eh?" he mused. "I have a sort of idea on that, but not a very exact one. Have you worked it out yet, chief?"

The Avenger nodded.

"Yes. I formed a pretty conclusive idea some time ago of just what must have been done. This confirms it."

The candle flared up, down, almost went out. Then the flame caught on the dregs of wax and steadied again.

"At the beginning, of course," said The Avenger, "it was necessary to start with pure theory. Not only power plants, but *all* electrical generating systems, on cars and farms and boats, everything, went dead. What could conceivably cause such a universal stoppage of units having nothing whatever to do with each other? There was only one theoretical answer.

"It could be accomplished only by somehow short-circuiting, in given areas, the constant electrical power of the earth, itself.

"As you know, the earth is really a gigantic generating unit. Whirling in space, it creates power. When we turn a generator rapidly and generate power, we are in reality trapping part of this earth-generated electricity. Now, if that fundamental power could be diverted from a given area, in other words, if a section of earth could be short-circuited, within that area no electrical unit would work. Power could not be generated, no matter how fast our generators turned, because they'd be turning in a sort of electrical vacuum."

"Mon, 'tis an impossibility ye're talkin' of," protested MacMurdie.

"It would seem so," Dick said. "Yet, it was done. Till now, I have been unable to figure out quite how. But these drums, and Burton's mumble of some chemical, provide the answer. It would seem that fundamental chemistry has at last merged with fundamental physics in the shape of electricity.

"To stop Plant 4, Nevlo set up a spire, or discharge point, on either side of the building, bracketing it. I imagine these points were, and are, concealed in tall trees on the crest of each bank forming the gorge through which Marville River runs. These two poles *are both positive*, which means that earth's electrical current, gathered at the two points instead of bridging the gap, repels itself and cuts off that small section entirely. An electrical vacuum—"

"But what," said Smitty, jaws open with amazement, "could bring earth's current to a focal point at each of the two poles?"

"This chemical in the drums we're sitting on," said Benson evenly. "As I said, it seems that fundamental chemistry has merged with fundamental laws of electricity. Nevlo somehow found a chemical that brings to a focal point all the electricity in the vicinity. I should have known that before now. Needles—*with roots*. The needles, of course, are the poles set up for the short-circuiting. The roots are cables going down to this chemical buried in the earth—the earth being represented, in the diagram Janet Weems described, as a wavy line under the needle. The lines from the needle's tip represented lines of force. Specifically, in the case of the last power blackout, one needle, or pole, was the radio tower at Portland. The other was the radio tower at Los Angeles, with a confederate doing the work out there. These two poles shorted earth's power over a continent till the terrific current burned out the ground cable, the drum in the earth containing the chemical, and the tips of the towers themselves. The radio power tubes, of course, blew at the first touch."

Smitty shook his head in something like awe.

"That's the biggest achievement of the century," he said. "Nevlo must have been a genius before his accident."

"Yes, a genius. But a warped genius. For this thing, mighty as it is, is entirely destructive. It can be used for no constructive purpose whatever. It was of value only as a tremendous lever with which to pry blackmail out of the utilities corporations."

"And we're sittin' on a similar arrangement, now?" demanded Mac, staring apprehensively at the drums.

"Yes," said The Avenger, voice as calm as his icy, colorless eyes.

"It doesn't seem to be working," said Smitty.

"I imagine," Dick said, "that the chemical, unaltered, is static and does not function. It would have to be that way, or it could not be handled at all; you can't carry drums around with all earth's lightning coursing through your body. To perform its task, the chemical must need the final addition of some other element. Perhaps another chemical, perhaps mere moisture."

Smitty didn't like his next question, because he really knew the answer in advance. But he asked it, anyway.

"Why are we roosting on drums of the stuff?"

Benson's eyes and tone continued to be as calm as if he were discussing the weather.

"We have meddled in this blackmail plan. So we are to be liquidated. We are to be electrocuted, with Mother Earth, herself, providing the current. The copper cable overhead, no doubt, leads out to one of Nevlo's power spires. At some moment in the near future, this chemical will be made to function. Earth will be short-circuited in this small area, through these drums."

"Well," said Smitty, "you can't even guess at the millions of volts that'll stream up and away from each other through Nevlo's needles. But I know one thing. That copper cable, thick as it is, won't begin to carry the load."

The Avenger said nothing. Smitty went reluctantly on with his train of thought.

"So," he said, "when the show commences, cable and drums and everything else will be almost instantly consumed by the gigantic electrical overload."

"Hey," said Mac, "and what becomes of *us*?"

"We'll be cinders, only you won't be able to find us," said Smitty. "Neat way of disposing of bodies, I'd say."

"So this is what the workman who died on our threshold wanted to tell us," said Mac, veering away from the personal angle. "He'd got a hint of the thing. And Burton, the new engineer, had caught a glimpse of the secret. He was blown up in his car. Janet Weems got through, but was shocked out of her mind—"

The sound of steps stopped him. A man came into the cave.

"Hi, pals," he said to the bound three. "Havin' a good time?"

"You'll have a better one, ye skurlie, if we ever get loose," grated Mac.

"You won't get loose," said the man. "Or your buddies, either. You're goin' to go up in smoke, in about three minutes. I don't know how it's done, but I do know it works!"

The man was carrying a can with a long spout on it.

"What's in the can?" asked Benson, voice calm and cold and even.

The man stared curiously, and a little fearfully, at The Avenger. Then he shrugged.

"Water, if it'll do you any good to know," he said. "Just plain aqua that you wash your hands in."

In each of the three steel drums there was a plug near the top. The man unscrewed these with a wrench. Into the holes he inserted the spout, pouring a third of his bucketful of water into each drum. He didn't bother to put the plugs back.

He was just withdrawing the spout from the third drum, Smitty's drum, when the candle gave a final flare, then went out.

His laugh sounded in the darkness.

"So long, pals. As soon as this stuff gets soaked clear to the bottom, and as soon as the big shot outside makes contact, all your troubles will be over."

His steps, accelerated a little as if he were afraid the

146

drums would explode or something, sounded to the mouth of the small cave and out.

The three couldn't hear anything at all in the dark.

CHAPTER XVII

Blue Flame!

Smitty was first to say something. The giant's voice was measured and even. Smitty didn't want to die. But he, and every one of The Avenger's little band, knew that his number would have to be up eventually.

This was it!

Smitty could hear Mac thumping around on his drum, trying to get loose. Smitty wasn't trying that any more. As he had found out in a dozen previous attempts, even his gigantic strength couldn't break those bonds.

"I wonder," said Mac sourly, "how long it takes all this stuff underneath us to get thoroughly soaked."

"That guy said something about a contact to be made outside, too," said Smitty. "A big master switch of some kind, I suppose."

There was a sound of footsteps again. Then a solid thump.

"Chief!" yelled Smitty, in sudden fear.

There was no answer.

"Muster Benson—" quavered Mac.

"The rats!" raged Smitty. "That guy with the bucket must have come back and socked the chief. Even tied up and in the dark, they're afraid of him. Hitting a guy when he can't hit back! If I could get my hands on them—"

" 'Tis just as well," said Mac somberly. "The chief might as well be unconscious when all this happens. Not that it'd make dyin' any easier for him. I've thought all along that he'd really like that, sort of. But it would make him so mad to think that for once he got licked by the human lice he hates so much—"

"Well!" said Smitty. "Seems to me you're singing a different tune. Licked, huh? A minute ago you said you were sure we'd get out of this."

"Well, I'm still sure," mumbled Mac, without conviction.

They sat in silence, then, unable to see each other, unable to see Dick Benson's unconscious form. They couldn't even see the barrels of death on which they sat.

With their eyes accustomed to pitch darkness, they could now see, at the entrance to the cave, a faint little flicker of light from a candle a long way off. Out there, somewhere, near the spot where that thick upper cable led . . .

The other end of the cable was nearly a hundred yards from the prison cave.

The cable ran down the tunnel roof to this spot, then went up into a narrow fissure in the rock roof. Presumably, it went on up to the surface and there contacted the foot of the steel spire, which was necessary to form a discharge point for the electricity focused by the chemical in the drums.

But between floor and roof, in the thick cable, was a yard-long gap. Slanted out from one end of this was a copper bar of just the right length to bridge the gap. When the bar was placed across the gap, the circuit would be completed, just as a circuit is completed when a conventional switch is thrown. So that, in effect, this copper bar was a master switch.

The handle of the switch was ten feet long, insulated over all its length. The current to flow along the bar was obviously something to compel extreme respect.

Near the switch were nearly twenty men.

Any of the Avenger's crew, had they been there, would have recognized one of them. It was the man who had come running to the power plant with the tale of Nevlo's freak accident that had turned him into a gorilla-twisted madman. The rest were just a fine assortment of gangsters of the type you would instinctively turn to if you wanted a few orphans and widows machine-gunned.

There were two other men there. One was the gorilla himself, weaving around the rock floor in a sort of silly dance, with his arms in front of him like a wrestler. The second was evident only as a voice. The owner sat on a rock off to one side in the shadows, so that he looked almost like part of the rock himself.

"We'll give it another few minutes," this one said in incisive, authoritative tones. "We want to be sure the chemical is completely ready. Probably it's ready, now, but I don't know the exact time required after pouring in the water."

The men looked with varying degrees of curiosity at the impromptu master switch to be thrown in a minute. But there was one expression on their faces that didn't show any variation. It was the same with all.

That was a sort of supernatural fear.

Every one of them had dealt death to a fellow human. But it was the kind of death a gangster could understand—via gun, knife or bomb. Now, in a moment, one of their number would move the switch, and three men would go up in blue flame! The weirdness of it awed them.

Two candles gave light in this larger cave at the far end of the copper conduit. Evidently, the figure in shadow, with face and body unidentifiable, could see the luminous hands of his watch.

He said: "One minute more—"

The candles went out.

They did not go out simultaneously. First one went out; then, after about two seconds, the other went out. Preceding each little death of light, there was a tiny *spattt* of sound no louder than if someone had snapped a small twig.

"Hey, there must be a draft in here," called one of the men near the copper cable.

"Light up again," ordered the voice of the man who had been in shadow.

There was a pause, shuffling steps, the rasp of a hand over rock.

"I can't find the damn things," complained a voice.

"You dumbbell, don't you carry matches?"

A match flared.

"I still can't find 'em," said the man. "I'd have sworn they were right here—"

"Never mind," said the man off to one side. "Throw that switch."

"You're sure *we* won't get it in the neck?" said one of the gang uneasily.

"Of course, I'm sure. Stay a few feet away from the switch, that's all."

The men all huddled at the end of the cave, not far from the man who spoke—except the one who was to throw the switch.

"Go on, go on!" snarled the man off to one side. "There's nothing to fear. It's the chemical that's dangerous, and that's three or four feet away in another cave, with those meddlers who work with Benson sitting on it."

"Okay, then," said the man, reaching far out to grasp the switch. "Here goes—"

"*Wait!*"

The word was not loud in the darkness. But it seemed to fill the cave with the icy crackle of authority. And it seemed to come from everywhere at once.

"What the hell—"

The man who had been hunting for the candles lit another match. It revealed the huddle of men not far from the switch—and that was all.

"I'd have sworn that was that guy Benson," said somebody nervously.

"It was," came the glacial voice.

"He's in *here!*"

"Don't let your imaginations run away with you," the man off to one side snarled icily. "Benson is in the next cave. There must be some trick of acoustics by which he can hear from out there and make us hear him."

"I hope you're right," said one of the men. "What you want, Benson?" He raised his voice, as if to call to far distances.

The answer came in a voice not raised at all.

"I want to tell you not to throw that switch."

The men milled around in the darkness. Now and then one lit a match, but the little glare didn't illuminate anything more than a yard or so away.

There was a thumping sound, and footsteps, then silence. The men lit matches frantically, but could see nothing.

"I am giving you just this one warning," came the cold, measured voice, like the voice of doom itself. "Don't try to destroy us by throwing that switch. If you do, you will never live to regret it."

"*Bah!*" snapped the man who was leader here. "It's a stupid trick to try to delay things. Throw the switch."

There was a silence, no click of bar meeting conduit. The man at the switch wasn't awfully anxious to act.

"Throw that switch, I say!"

"Look, boss," came the voice of the man commanded.

"I've heard a lot about this Avenger guy and the way he works. Try to kill him, and you only kill yourself. It's happened before—"

"Damn you all for a pack of cowards," raged the man. "I'll throw it myself. Get out of my way!"

There were crisp, purposeful steps in the blackness.

"Chief!" said Mac again.

No answer.

"Guess he's still out," sighed Smitty. "And I guess we don't go on calling to him, or doing anything else, much longer. This stuff we're on must be soaked plenty."

"Wonder what it is," said Mac. The Scot, even at this moment on the brink of death, was irked that he couldn't guess at the nature of the chemical. After all, Mac was one of the best chemists in America. He felt he should have been able to guess.

"Whatever it is," said Smitty, straining at his bonds in the darkness, even though he knew it was useless, "it's a shame the government hasn't got a supply in its secret War Department vaults. It could certainly fix any invading enemy right up."

"If Muster Benson had only had a chance," bemoaned Mac. "But that Nevlo must have met him at the bottom of the chute with a club, just like he met us—"

"*Mac!*" yelled Smitty.

For suddenly the world had gone up in a blinding flash of blue flame!

It was by far the strongest at the entrance to their cave. But it penetrated the farthest corner, like lightning. It seemed to break through the closed eyelids of the two men and sear their brains.

Then it died. And with it died all sound. There had been a confusion of yells in the far distance outside. But now these had disappeared.

There was just the dark and the terrible silence.

"*Whoosh!*" moaned Mac. "Smitty, we're dead."

There was no answer.

"*Smitty!*"

The silence persisted.

"I always said he didn't live right," moaned Mac. "I've gone to heaven, and he's gone to the other place. Poor Smitty—"

"Shut up, you chump!" snapped the giant. "I hear something. Somebody coming toward us. At least, I think I do. If you'll just stop your caterwauling—"

"But we're dead, Smitty. We must be. Somebody threw the switch outside, and there was that blue flame."

"The flame came from the cave outside here, you Scotch raven," barked Smitty. "It didn't come from this cave at all. The drums we're on are all right, and we're all right. And I'll swear I heard steps."

"You did," came a voice from the cave mouth. It was The Avenger's voice.

"*Chief!*" yelled Smitty.

There was a flickering light, which rounded the corner and entered the little cave. The light came from a candle in a steely, slim hand. It flared upward, illuminating, as in an amber spotlight, Dick Benson's face.

"We thought ye'd got socked in the darkness by that guy," said Mac almost tearfully. "We thought maybe ye were dead. And ourselves, too, to be frank about it."

"It's the others who are dead," said The Avenger.

He cut the two loose.

In the larger cave outside, Smitty and Mac stared with chilling blood at a spectacle never seen before on earth—and probably never to be seen again.

The spectacle of over a score of men after they had been transfixed by all the mighty voltage of this area of earth's surface.

There had been a huddle of the men away from the cable at the far end of the cave. There was nothing recognizably human left. That whole end of the cavern presented a bluish, fused look where tremendous power had flared.

There was no sign of copper cable or of the switch bar. In the rock of the floor, a perfect circle was fused, where a steel drum had been standing, a drum consumed to the last atom in the blue flame.

At this terrible scene, the pale eyes of The Avenger stared broodingly.

"I told them not to do it," he said, voice so low it could scarcely be heard. "I warned them."

Smitty cleared his throat and stared at the things that had been men. The things varied in size according to the distance they'd been from the drum.

There were a few cindery objects almost half as big as bodies. But most of the gnarled black lumps were no larger than a skull, while a few were scarcely fist-size.

And where the switch had been, there was nothing at all. Not one trace to tell that a man had stood there.

Smitty stared at The Avenger.

"I cut loose with Ike, in the darkness," Benson said, tone still brooding and low.

"We thought you'd been slugged. We heard a thump—"

"That must have been when I broke the copper cable fastened to the ceiling of our cave. I broke it near the drums, took the broken end, and bent it out the cave door.

"Then I came back and got the drum I'd been sitting on. I carried that out, too, as near to the men as I could without getting in the light of their candles. I shot the candles out with Mike, then carried the drum over near where they were. After that, I connected the broken end of the cable once more to the drum."

Smitty exclaimed loudly, "So that when the switch was thrown, the current went right through them instead of us!"

"That's right," said Benson.

Mac stared at the little black lumps that had been men

—if you wanted to call professional killers men.

"Which one of these was Nevlo?" he asked.

"None of them," said The Avenger.

The two stared quickly at him.

"There wasn't any Nevlo," said Benson. "I suspected that from the start, and the suspicion was confirmed when you, Smitty, found that body under the floor of Plant 4."

"But I—" began the giant, bewildered.

"The body had a curiously deformed neck. The muscles of the left side were a little withered. That indicated that it was Nevlo, who held his head habitually to the left, from descriptions we got. And the body showed signs of torture.

"Nevlo was a great engineer. He discovered this chemical principle of creating an electrical vacuum. With it, he rendered Plant 4 useless out of pure vindictiveness. Blake saw further. He—"

"*Blake?*" said Smitty.

"Yes, he's the one responsible for the wholesale power failures. In Nevlo's petty use of a mighty secret he saw a chance to get untold millions through its use on a vaster scale. No one was able to 'find' Nevlo for weeks. That was because Blake had found him first. Had found him, tortured him unmercifully to get his secret from him, then killed him and hid his body in the convenient trench in the powerhouse floor, after decapitating him to make his identification impossible. Then he went ahead blackmailing the power barons. One, it seemed, wouldn't knuckle under. That was Hooley, of Bar Harbor, who was murdered."

"If Nevlo's body is under the powerhouse floorrr," said Mac, "who played the part of Nevlo later?"

"I don't know," said Benson. "That is, I don't know his name or identity. But I know the type. He was some broken-down, punch-drunk prize fighter or wrestler Blake picked up. The man was dim-witted, foolish, but just sane enough to take orders and follow them. Probably, Blake introduced him to his henchmen as Nevlo. He needed a Nevlo, you see, to be the mouthpiece for his blackmail demands, so he himself wouldn't be suspected by the other power magnates."

"You knew that as far back as the time when the power gang met in Cleveland," accused Smitty.

"I accepted it as probable," said Benson. "I didn't quite *know* it. But I made up as Nevlo, entered the conference of power executives, and learned there that Blake was actually the ringleader."

"How'd you get onto the guy?" said Smitty.

"I named a blackmail sum, ridiculously small," said Dick. "Five million dollars. It might just as easily have been fifty million. And some such sum, no doubt, was what Blake had coached his ferocious moron to say. When he heard his follower say five million, he gave himself away. The rest showed relief at the smallness of the amount. But he gasped with anger and amazement. For just a second his face was an open book."

The Avenger stared at the spot where Blake had stood when he had thrown the switch. If you knew just where to look, you could see a curious little button of metal on the rock floor, an amalgam formed by a gold crown, several silver dental fillings, and a gold pocketknife. That was all.

A supercrook had perished by his own hand and taken his cutthroat hirelings to hell with him when he sought to destroy The Avenger. That was ever The Avenger's way. Another battle against crime had been won, at a moment when all had seemed to be lost.

But Mac and Smitty, staring covertly at their chief, knew that it was only another chapter concluded, not the end of the book.

"Arnold and his men will be somewhere outside, searching for an entrance into the caves," Dick said quietly. "Go and find them, Smitty. Bring them back here. They can chalk this up to the credit of their bureau, and also take away those drums you and Mac sat on. The War Department will want those, to give an enemy who might some day want to set foot on our shores a most unpleasant surprise."

YOU AIN'T READ NOTHIN' YET UNTIL YOU'VE READ

JOLSON

by Michael Freedland

78-200 / $1.50

He called himself "the world's greatest entertainer"... and no one could deny it.

He was born the son of an orthodox Russian Jewish Cantor and became the toast of Broadway, the husband of Ruby Keeler, friend of Presidents, singer of the early songs of Berlin and Gershwin, the man who gave the movies their voice.

This is the story of Al Jolson: the immortal story of the "Jazz Singer" who taught the world to swing!

"... a labor of love."—*Book-of-the-Month-Club News*
"Warm, gossipy."—*Pittsburgh Press*
"Nostalgic ... bittersweet."—*Publishers Weekly*
"Incisive."—*Chicago Tribune*

DON'T MISS

JOLSON

WARNER PAPERBACK LIBRARY

A Warner Communications Company
Wherever Paperbacks Are Sold